Beyond The Dark Tower

Illustrated by Joseph Vargo

Written by Joseph Vargo and Joseph Iorillo
Monolith Graphics, Cleveland, Ohio

Published By Monolith Graphics
Cleveland, Ohio
www.monolithgraphics.com

Cover and Interior Artwork by Joseph Vargo
Graphic Design by Christine Filipak

Publisher's Cataloging-in-Publication Data
Beyond The Dark Tower / by Joseph Vargo and Joseph Iorillo
ISBN(13): 9780982489925
1. Fiction—Horror 2. Vampires
3. Ghost Stories I. Vargo, Joseph

First Edition
Printed and Published in the United States of America

Herein lie the dark legends scribed long ago, unearthed and translated from ancient scrolls and arcane tomes. These tragic tales of myth and forbidden lore chronicle a sinister legacy, as it unfolded in the forgotten past, and the curse that yet lurks within the shadow of The Dark Tower.

Contents

Crusaders

JOSEPH VARGO

High above the small village of Merkova, the heavens rumbled ominously as monstrous thunderclouds billowed and churned, consuming the daylight in writhing blackness. The gathering tempest erupted furiously, unleashing violent waves of rain that pelted the meager hovels like an unending torrent of arrows. The dull thud of heavy hoof beats rose above the sounds of the storm as six riders followed the muddy road that led from the forest to the town's northern edge. The galloping steeds slowed to a steady trot as they sloshed through the bog of deep puddles covering the narrow cobblestone path until, at last, they came to a halt before the iron gates of the village graveyard.

Five of the riders wore heavy chainmail and armor, bearing the same cross-shaped insignia etched into their tarnished breastplates, marking them as knights of some unknown sacred order. The battle-scarred longswords at their sides silently affirmed that they were veteran warriors who had been tested by combat. The sixth man was cloaked in the simple robes of a monk, his face concealed in the shadows of a thick black hood. As the knights surveyed the graveyard and village structures, the holy man whispered a Latin prayer and caressed a wooden crucifix that hung from a chain around his neck.

The downpour diminished to a steady rain that created an eerie fog throughout the village and surrounding woodlands, enveloping the crusaders in an aura of gloom. As the creeping mist descended upon them, the knights dismounted and tethered their steeds to the rust-worn rails of the cemetery gate. After quickly removing a curious array of gear and weapons from their saddles and packs, the armored soldiers entered the forsaken graveyard and proceeded to span outward, following separate paths. The priest turned his attention to the paltry huts and hovels that comprised the village and walked to a nearby dwelling where he pounded his fist on the rickety pine door.

After a moment the door opened slowly and an old man peered out from the dimly lit room. "Yes?" The elderly man clutched the door tightly in an effort to steady his trembling hands.

A coarse voice emanated from the shadows of the monk's cowl. "I am Father Aldis from the priory of Vestus."

"Welcome father," the man replied, a noticeable hint of relief in his voice, "welcome to our village and to my humble home. Please, please—step inside to escape the downpour." The old man hobbled aside, allowing his guest to enter the small house. "I am Nestor, and this is my nephew Kristoff." He motioned to a younger man, sitting quietly at a simple wooden table behind him.

Once inside, the holy man threw back the hood of his robe, revealing his gaunt countenance and shaven head. Though he did not possess the rugged physique or brutish features of his comrades, the priest's eyes held the solemn stare of a man who had witnessed much tragedy in his life. "We have come in response to reports that a child from this region has gone missing."

The two village men exchanged nervous glances, then Nestor spoke again, "I mean no disrespect my lord, but may I ask why this matter has roused the interest of the royal guard?

"We are not the royal guard," Aldis answered. "We serve

a higher power. Our mission is to investigate all matters that provoke our suspicions—to determine whether unholy powers may be to blame. There is a blight upon this land and we have been sanctioned to seek it out and destroy it, wherever it has taken root. The prey that we hunt has a penchant for the blood of innocents."

A wild look filled the younger man's eyes as he rose from his seat. "It is as I have told you!" Kristoff exclaimed, rushing forward and falling to his knees before the priest. "Bless us Father! Bless us and save us from damnation, for the Devil has set upon us! He has claimed two souls since the last new moon. First, the holy man went missing, then my own daughter was snatched from her bed while she slept."

Retaining his composure, the priest helped Kristoff to his feet and spoke to him in a quiet, consoling tone. "Tell me of your daughter."

"Her name is Lena. She is a sweet child. No one would ever wish to do her harm." Tears welled in Kristoff's eyes as he continued. "She vanished from her bed three nights ago, and no one has seen her since. We have searched the village and surrounding forests. We have scoured the wells and riverbanks but have found no trace of her."

"Have there been any sightings of wolves?"

"It is no wolf that plagues us," Kristoff whispered. "I have seen the beast's vile shadow in the graveyard at night. The demon that stalks us walks as a man."

The priest's eyes narrowed. "You have said that your holy man has disappeared as well?"

"Yes, on the night of the new moon—the eve of the Sabbath."

"Tell me more of this," Aldis calmly demanded.

The elderly Nestor responded. "He had performed mass

earlier in the day and was seen by several townsfolk just before dusk. When night came, the darkness carried something foul into our village. Horses and goats stirred in their stables, and dogs barked and growled at empty shadows. The next day, some spoke of hearing screams in the night. We set forth to the chapel to seek the holy man's guidance, but he was not to be found."

As the priest pondered the old man's words, one of the armor-clad soldiers rushed to the open door. "Father Aldis," the young knight exclaimed, "Stephon has found something among the graves."

Without a word, the priest turned and quickly followed the messenger outside. Nestor and Kristoff remained in the doorway and watched the pair vanish into the eerie fog as they passed through the rusted gates that marked the threshold of the dead.

The knight hurriedly led Aldis along a muddy path that twisted through an overgrown field filled with crooked tombstones and crude wooden crosses. In the distance, the silhouetted forms of four armored men stood motionless in the mist like statues of angels gathered around a stone crypt built into a small hillside. In his long months of service with them, the priest had come to feel a deep kinship with his fellow crusaders, not unlike the bond shared among brothers. He trusted each of them with his life and respected their formidable skills.

As he drew closer, Aldis could distinguish the stern faces of his comrades. Edwin, Ian and Thomas held loaded crossbows and stood in a semicircle with their backs to the crypt while Stephon stared intently at the tomb, his right hand firmly gripping the hilt of his sword. Aldis stopped beside the silent sentinel and followed his unblinking gaze.

"It is as we suspected," Stephon declared grimly.

The doors of the crypt gaped open as if they had been torn asunder by some unearthly force. Mud seeped into the open tomb, creeping down the weathered stone steps in a thick, ruddy ooze.

As they stood contemplating the sight before them, another form approached swiftly through the fog. Before the shadow was upon them, the knights instinctively took defensive action. Thomas tackled the unknown intruder and threw him to the ground as Ian and Edwin drew their swords and prepared to strike.

"Wait!" Father Aldis ordered, stepping forward to assess the threat.

Thomas clutched his captive by the throat, holding him in place on the muddy ground as the priest stood over them. Aldis cast his gaze upon the intruder, recognizing the forlorn face of Kristoff and quickly realizing that the grieving father had run after them, following them to the grave.

"Please," Kristoff uttered, gasping for breath, "I must know."

The priest nodded his head and Thomas relinquished his grip.

Kristoff stared in horror at the open tomb as he slowly rose to his feet. A look of revulsion and dread filled his eyes as he asked, "What does it mean?"

The priest looked back toward the yawning crypt and spoke solemnly. "The quarry we hunt carries the Devil's taint. Such creatures cannot withstand the divine rays of God's sunlight. Its radiance is blinding to them and its slightest caress sears the flesh from their bones. During the hours of daylight, these vile fiends must seek refuge underground, deep in the earth, where they rest safe among the dead."

"And what of Lena?" Kristoff sobbed, "What has become of my daughter?"

The priest stared blankly at him, offering no consolation or answer, then turned and descended the steps of the tomb. The knights followed closely behind him, wary of every sound and movement as they entered the violated gravesite. Once within the musty confines of the stone vault, the crusaders lit torches, sending shadows scurrying to cower in the tomb's furthest recesses. The priest's eyes quickly darted around the empty chamber until his gaze came to rest on a small bundle lying on the floor. He picked up a knotted piece of twine that held a wooden trinket, crudely carved in the shape of a bird.

Father Aldis turned to face Kristoff, who stood just outside the entrance to the crypt.

Fighting back tears, Kristoff acknowledged his recognition of the simple bauble in the priest's hand. "It is my daughter's necklace," he said quietly.

Thomas' voice cut through the gloom like a sword. "Here," he said, pointing to an opening in the stones of the far wall.

Aldis stepped to the fractured wall and thrust his torch into the gaping hole to reveal a low tunnel within. "They have taken her," he whispered.

"No!" the girl's father screamed.

Aldis turned to address his comrades. "These are no animals acting on savage instinct. There is wile and forethought in this. I am now most certain of it. They took the village priest first, then the girl. They knew we would come, and this necklace was surely left here for us to discover."

"But why?" Edwin asked, unable to comprehend any rationale in their adversary's actions.

"To draw us into their lair," Stephon declared, his growling voice sending resonant echoes throughout the hollow crypt.

Thomas withdrew his longsword. "Then so be it."

Aldis put his hand on the sword's blade and lowered it to the ground then stepped between the knights and the opening in the wall, blocking the tunnel's entrance. "Let us not rush blindly to our deaths." The holy man spoke quietly as he imparted his wisdom with a persuasive grace. "The foes we now face are no mindless thralls." He gestured his free hand toward the opening behind him. "Surely they await us in the shadows within." Aldis paused for a long moment, locking eyes with each of his comrades. Their clenched jaws and furled brows revealed no hint of fear. As the priest's eyes met with Stephon's, the holy man recognized the seething fury that raged behind the knight's steely gaze. At last, Aldis said, "Let us prepare to meet our hosts properly."

The priest removed a leather pouch that hung at his side then said a prayer as he anointed the knights' weapons with blessed oil, coating each blade and arrow with a dark fluid that was venomous to the ranks of the unholy. When he had finished delivering his benediction, Father Aldis laid a firm but gentle hand on Kristoff's shoulder, saying, "Stay here. If your daughter yet lives, we shall find her and bring her back to you."

The village man clutched his daughter's necklace and watched as one by one the crusaders stepped through the small crevice in the stone wall and disappeared into the shadows beyond.

The holy warriors emerged within a narrow tunnel carved though dirt and clay, lined with rotting timbers and human bones. They proceeded slowly, in single file, letting the winding passageway lead them deep below the field of graves. After a short while, the tunnel opened into a natural cavern in the bedrock beneath the village. There were no signs of life, save for scattered swarms of bats that stirred in the heights of the cavernous tunnel.

As they continued their search, they wound deeper into the earth, and the droning rumble of the storm was muffled to an eerie hush. After a short while, the unnerving silence was broken by the distant sound of weeping. The faint cries led them to a circular chamber in the heart of the cavern. The vaulted walls were reinforced by crudely chiseled bricks, and stone archways supported six passageways leading away from the chamber in different directions. Louder and more distinct, the sobbing cries echoed from a shadowy archway that framed a tunnel on the opposite side of the chamber. The crusaders trained their crossbows on the darkened passageway and stood their ground as the sounds drew closer. They watched in silence as a young girl slowly emerged from the pitch black of the tunnel and stopped beneath the archway. She stood before them, holding her hands in front of her face to shield her eyes from the light of their torches.

"Lena?" Aldis called.

The girl slowly lowered her hands, revealing her withered face. Dark circles surrounded the child's sunken eyes and her lips were the color of dried blood. Stephon took a step toward the girl, but Father Aldis raised his hand to stop him. "No," he ordered curtly, "wait."

The priest opened a small flask then held out his crucifix and cast holy water at the girl. As soon as the first drop touched her flesh, the girl recoiled in agony and let loose an inhuman shriek.

"She is wampior!" Thomas yelled.

Faster than the eye could follow, the demon child leapt across the room and pounced upon Edwin, knocking him to the ground. She seized the knight's throat with her claw-like fingers, digging her nails beneath his flesh, and tore the veins from his neck, sending a cascade of blood to cover the floor. Ian fired a shot from his crossbow, but the girl moved too swiftly, darting into the shadows and narrowly evading the blessed arrow's deadly kiss. Thomas cast his torch into the darkened alcove where the girl had disappeared, and the firelight revealed her frail form cowering in the shadows. With one stride the creature leapt high onto the wall, clinging to the chiseled bricks with her talons. She let loose a shrill wail, causing dozens of bats to flee their resting places in the chamber's heights. The screeching bats surrounded the crusaders in a flurry of wings and shadows. As the descending swarm engulfed them, the knights swatted at the loathsome creatures with their swords and torches. After their swift assault, the swarm dispersed, fleeing the chamber through the various tunnels that surrounded the room, but the swirling confusion had caused the vampire hunters to lose sight of their quarry.

Stephon squinted into the darkened heights of the chamber, scanning the shadows for the unholy creature that had killed his friend. "Where is she?" he demanded.

The remaining knights held their torches high, but the meager firelight could not illuminate the full extent of the caverns above them. The crusaders stood in silence, surveying the shadowy perimeter of the chamber, listening and watching for the slightest sound or movement. Stephon peered into the bleak depths of the dark tunnels that surrounded them, uncertain of which one had led them into the chamber, and realized that he and his comrades had been lured into a deadly trap.

A sound similar to a serpent's hiss drew the crusaders' attention to a darkened archway beyond Edwin's lifeless body. As the knight's turned to face whatever had made the sound, Father Aldis took a step back, raising his crucifix before him. While the holy warriors held their vigilant positions and stared into the ominous void, Lena silently emerged from the shadows above them, slowly crawling down the wall behind the priest. She crept along the stones without notice then stopped a few feet above the holy man and readied to strike. The vampiric child reached down toward the unsuspecting priest, her deadly talons within inches of his throat. Before the creature could strike, Thomas detected her descending shadow in the periphery of his vision and reacted without hesitation, whirling and firing his crossbow at the demon child. The quarrel hit its mark dead-center, penetrating the girl's chest and piercing her heart.

Lena dropped to the ground hissing and shrieking as Stephon leapt to her side. The knight held the girl's neck beneath his armored boot, crushing her throat to the ground as Father Aldis emptied his flask of holy water onto her writhing body. Lena's pale flesh began to blister and smoke where the sacred water fell upon her. Ian withdrew a large iron spike from his pack and pressed the tip to the girl's chest just beside the half-buried crossbow bolt. Thomas stood over the girl, raising a large hammer over his head with both hands. Amidst a cacophony of inhuman shrieks, the priest quickly delivered the girl's last rites then made the sign of the cross and nodded woefully to Thomas. The knight brought the sledge down with all his might, driving the spike through the girl's torso and deep into the earth below. The demon child relinquished a final gasp then, at last, her body fell still. After a moment of silence, Stephon took a step back and lowered his torch to the girl's body, setting her lifeless corpse ablaze.

Knowing that their gruesome work was not yet finished, Aldis turned away. He had witnessed the ritual countless times, and though he understood the necessity of the knight's actions, taking part in the deeds sickened him. He closed his eyes and whispered a prayer to himself, but the priest could not distract his mind from the horrific thoughts of what would follow. After the girl's corpse had been sanctified by fire, her heart would be removed and her head would be severed. Then, regrettably, they would repeat the ritual with the body of their fallen comrade.

As the vampire slayers were engrossed in their grisly work, another sound caught Father Aldis' ear. A low whisper, perhaps a draft of wind, resonated from the shadowed arch behind him. He cautiously followed the sound down a darkened passage, hoping to find a path to the surface, but instead the tunnel came to a halt before an ancient tomb. The stone slab that had been used to seal the vault had been pushed inward and the doorway now gaped open.

The whisper came again and this time Aldis clearly heard it call his name. He thrust his torch through the crypt's entrance, but the flame's light seemed to be consumed by the darkness within. Hesitantly, he entered the ancient burial chamber, regretting his foolish act before he could stop himself. As soon as he stepped through the opening, the tomb door began to slide closed. Aldis turned to run, but he lost his footing and stumbled in the darkness, dropping his torch in the dirt. Before the stone door closed completely, an armored figure leapt through the narrowing gap. It was Stephon. The heavy slab crushed the knight's torch, snapping it in two as he tumbled to the ground inside the tomb. The door crashed shut, sealing both men within the dim confines of the burial vault.

Low laughter preceded a raspy voice that emanated from the shadows. "Welcome brother, how long has it been?" The voice, though no more than a low, coarse whisper, was one that was somehow familiar to Father Aldis. A shape stepped forward, silhouetted by the shadows of the crypt and two eyes caught the reflection of the torchlight to glisten in the darkness.

Aldis squinted to focus on the dark form that stood before him. Though he could not see the figure's face, he recognized the voice as that of a fellow priest from his order. "Drago? Is it truly you? What has happened to you?"

"I have been enlightened, old friend." There was a distinct tone of mocking in the shadow's voice as the dark figure cast something onto the torch that lay burning on the ground.

Aldis peered deeply into the flame and was aghast to see a silver crucifix smoldering in the fire.

"We were wrong to rest our faith in such humbling practices," the grim voice continued. "At long last, I have found true salvation."

Stephon remained silent, surveying their dire situation. The walls were solid stone and they were far below the surface of the graveyard. The granite slab that sealed the entrance was too heavy to be moved by a single man. If the tomb held any other exits, they were on the other side of the chamber. They would have to cross the room, and they would have to get past their captor to escape.

The shadow spoke again. "It was I who summoned thee here."

"Summoned us?" Aldis said, his mind unable to fathom the meaning of Drago's words. "Why?"

"To resolve the matters that remain unfinished between us. As you surely recall, it was I who originally had been chosen to accompany the crusaders on their sacred mission—the very mission that has brought thee here. We were close friends at one time, were we not?"

Aldis' voice was little more than a whisper. "Yes."

"Yet, when I fell ill, you did not hesitate to take my place. You offered no words of solace when you abandoned me in the monastery where I lay in fevered delirium. I thought of you often during my suffering. When at last I regained my health, you were gone and I was sent to this dismal, forsaken village to spend my days among these pitiful fools. I had committed no crime yet I was condemned to a desolate fate preaching to the deaf ears and shallow minds of wretches no better than the goats they tended. Listening to them confess their petty indiscretions and lustful urges drove me to the brink of madness, but I was rescued—by those who showed me the path of true salvation.

"I did not mean to abandon thee," Aldis replied, "I had no choice in the matter. You were deathly ill and thine duties fell upon me. Our parting was destined by fate."

"Fate?" Drago hissed, "Perhaps it was. Strange is it not? For certainly fate has brought us together once again. But I now hold thine fate in my hands, for those who have shown me the true path have given me the power to exact my vengeance."

"Nay, Drago—you are a mere pawn in the Devil's game. These foul creatures fear us. They have corrupted your mind and blinded thee from the truth. They care not whether you live or die."

"And will the gentle god of your myths and superstition care whether you live or die, my friend? Did your all-compassionate god prevent us from seizing that child? Perhaps you should ask yourself why there is so much darkness in the world and so little light."

The torch crackled as the flames grew dim.

"My queen fears no mortal man," Drago's said, his voice echoing menacingly, "for she commands the immortal legions of darkness. We are the shadows that haunt the blackest wells of midnight. You too shall learn to worship the Dark Queen, for she and she alone is our true savior."

"Blasphemy!" Aldis raised his voice to match Drago's rantings.

"Nay, old friend, I speak the truth. Those who join her are bestowed with her dark gifts—powers beyond mortal dreams—such as the power that now courses through my veins. But those who dare to stand against her shall be crushed beneath her wrath. She shall show them no mercy for their insolence. Even now, her legions are amassing within the ancient tower that looms beyond the village of Vasaria. They shall smite your pitiful crusaders as easily as thee would quash an army of toads.

"You shall soon discover the error of thine beliefs." The figure gestured to the sputtering torch lying on the ground. "When the flame dies, you shall be cast into darkness. I welcome the shadows, but you shall come to dread the ultimate blackness of my domain, the exalted blackness of the abyss."

"You shall know eternal darkness at the end of my blade," Stephon proclaimed boldly.

The figure's glistening eyes shifted to the knight. "Alas, the valiant protector to the end. Such virtue should be rewarded. I shall smite thee quickly to spare thee further torments."

As the flame from the priest's torch faded to a dim flicker, the shadow stepped forward and turned its head toward Father Aldis. "But I shall take my time with thee, old friend, so that we may reacquaint ourselves properly. I have much to share with thee."

The dark figure moved closer still, and now stood directly over the final glowing embers of the torch. Drago's face no longer bore the countenance of a man. His eyes were black as those of a raven and his mouth was lined with long, pointed teeth, sharp as the fangs of a serpent. His lips were gone, and his ashen face was distorted in a feral snarl.

Stephon acted without hesitation. In one swift motion, he tore Aldis' oil flask from his belt and slashed it with his dagger, then threw it onto Drago as he stood over the waning embers of the torch. The oil instantly ignited the creature's robes and within seconds Drago was ablaze and engulfed in blinding flames. A hellish wail erupted from the living inferno as it flailed and drew near. With lightning speed, Stephon spun and swung his longsword through the air, lopping off the creature's ghastly head in one clean slice. Still ablaze, the decapitated head tumbled to the ground, landing before the feet of Father Aldis.

Stephon remained silent as Aldis picked up the crucifix that Drago had discarded.

The priest's voice conveyed a mixture of anger and heartfelt sorrow for the loss of his friend. "He was a good man," he said quietly.

"Perhaps once, long ago," Stephon stared at the smoldering carcass that lay on the ground, "but this thing that lured us here was surely more devil than man."

Aldis stared at Drago's cross. The once-silver crucifix was now singed to black. "If a man of strong faith such as Drago can be corrupted and twisted into dark servitude, then what hope have we?"

Stephon laid a heavy hand upon his friend's shoulder. "In times of weakness all men can be tempted to stray from the righteous path." Stephon tightened his grip to add emphasis to the final part of his statement. "United, we remain strong."

The priest's gaze remained locked upon the tainted crucifix in his hand as he silently contemplated the knight's words.

"Come," Stephon said, "Let us not dwell here any longer."

An archway at the opposite end of the tomb opened into

a steep tunnel that led upward. The two men followed the path blindly until they emerged in a small mausoleum on the surface where the meager rays of daylight trickled through the rusted iron gates that sealed the crypt's entrance. With a well-placed kick of his armored boot, Stephon sent the ancient gates crashing open. Father Aldis followed the knight out into the misty graveyard beneath a cold drizzle of rain and the gloom of the overcast sky.

The priest took a deep breath of the cool air, relishing his narrow escape from the perils of the darkness below, then turned to face Stephon. "I owe you my life."

For a brief moment, the knight's rugged face almost betrayed a smile, then his eyes regained their icy stare. "Our mission is far from over," Stephon said. "We have much work to do."

"Yes," Aldis agreed, slipping Drago's tarnished crucifix over his head. "Let us gather our comrades and venture to the Tower beyond Vasaria." The priest cast his gaze toward the ominous clouds that stretched across the crimson skies to the East, then whispered a solemn vow, "Let us find this Dark Queen."

Night upon endless night do I languish here, longing to break free of the curse that binds me to this forsaken place. Yet here I remain, a slave to the Tower's call. For those who would follow in my path, I hereby relate my tragic tale.

A lifetime ago, I came to this ancient keep, unaware of its sinister history and blind to its ensnaring web. Had I but known the truth of the darkness that lurked here, or suspected the grim fate that awaited me, I would have fled these lands and lived a life free of woe. But I was heedless of the dangers as I ventured here, and now my penance seems without end.

I stand vigil over this forsaken keep and the undying darkness entombed beneath it—the Dark Queen, Mara, the murderous daughter of a forgotten king. Born of sorcery and dark deception, she grew to seize command of the Tower. Seduced by unholy powers, she was swayed to destroy all who opposed her. She sacrificed her humanity to become an immortal creature of darkness. Her empire spread to threaten all mankind, and as she stood on the verge of conquest, she and her loathsome horde were toppled by a holy man wielding a sacred blade.

This lone crusader found the strength to vanquish the Dark Queen, but only at the cost of his own soul, becoming a creature of darkness himself. He was the first to keep vigil here, guarding Mara's tomb so that she would not rise again. He became known as The Baron, and over the long years, he struggled against his affliction, denying his own consuming thirst for blood while he searched for the answers to his plight. He chronicled his discoveries and mad wisdom in a series of journals, in the hopes that his heirs might uncover the answers he so desperately sought.

When the Baron could resist his own dark desires no longer, fate brought me to the Tower. He passed his curse on to me, along with his vigil, and in turn, I ended his suffering. His sacred duties fell upon me. But I too found it impossible to resist my dark hungers. My own weakness led me to take the life of a village woman, Rianna, whom I loved dearly. She became a vessel for the Dark Queen's soul and Mara's wicked spirit was reborn within her. I ended her life, and I now seek salvation for her spirit.

I fear the Dark Queen will rise yet again, for her powers grow stronger and her followers are devoutly dedicated to freeing her black soul. I stand alone at the threshold of her earthly prison, sworn to stop her at any cost and send her wicked spirit to Hell. Only then will I find redemption. Only then will my soul be free.

The Witch of The Standing Stone

Joseph Vargo and Christine Filipak

The shrill cackle of ravens echoed through the mist-shrouded forest beneath the Dark Tower, splitting the dead of night. The raucous sound rose on the climbing wind to reach the Tower's heights, drawing the attention of the keep's vigilant guardian, Lord Brom. High atop the castle parapet, the Tower Lord stood among the fierce sentinels of stone, scanning the forest below. Spying the dim glow of candlelight in the dark woods, he swiftly descended through the Tower and ventured out into the forest to investigate the mysterious cause of the ravens' sudden unrest.

The ravens' shrieks led Brom to a long-forgotten hollow deep in the woods. As he approached the clearing his eyes beheld a halo of candlelight surrounding a beautiful young woman draped in a cloak of red velvet. The woman held her arms aloft as she chanted repeatedly, uttering some unknown incantation. Scores of ravens cried out from lofty perches among the barren branches of the encompassing trees. As Brom entered the hollow, the woman ceased her invocation and turned to face him. As she lowered her arms, the ravens fell silent.

The mysterious woman stood within a circle of seven candles set at points around a ring of strange symbols etched into the earth. A shimmering aura surrounded her velvet-clad form.

"Greetings, Lord Brom," the woman said, her voice soft

27

and hypnotic. Long flowing locks, red as the setting sun, framed her porcelain-white face. "I bid thee welcome."

Curious yet wary, Brom stepped toward her. He advanced to the edge of the circle on the ground, but could move no closer. Repelled by some unseen force, he could not penetrate the ring of arcane symbols.

A grin formed upon the woman's lips. "The mystic circle that surrounds me keeps me safe. No harm can befall me while I remain within its protective spell."

Brom took a step back into the shadows. "Your candles will not burn endlessly, witch. Your spell will not last forever."

"Nor shall the darkness of night, Lord Brom." She smiled again. "I am Daria of the wilds. As you have no doubt reasoned, our meeting on this night is no chance event." She gestured to the black birds that filled the surrounding trees. "I bade the ravens to summon thee here."

Brom stared deeply into her emerald eyes, recognizing the fire of enchantment burning within them. "For what purpose?" he asked.

"To share a tale with you, Lord Brom—one that has never been told to anyone outside my bloodline. It was told to me by my mother, as her mother told it to her. We have kept this secret safe among our own and passed it on for countless generations."

"Why tell it now?"

"I know of your quest to discover the ancient history of the Tower," Daria replied. "This tale will illuminate the shadows."

"I have little faith in the words of a sorceress," Brom declared gruffly.

"I speak the truth." Daria's voice held a tone of humble sincerity. "I know of your fearsome strength and power, my lord. I would not dare to make an enemy of one such as you."

Brom kept his unblinking stare fixed upon her. "Tell me,

then, what shall be gained by sharing your secret with me?"

Daria's head dropped and her hands ran across her stomach, directing Brom's attention to her swollen belly. "I am with child and shall soon give birth to my own daughter. When this happens, I shall lose much of my power. I wish to aid you in your mission to battle the dark forces that threaten us all, by revealing the origins of the evil that dwells here, so that you may better understand the nature of your enemy. I do this now so that my daughter might live free of the sinister shadow that has loomed over our people for far too long. I wish for my child to know a better world."

Daria lifted her head and a single tear ran down her smooth cheek. "If you will permit me, my lord, I shall reveal all I know."

"Very well," Brom whispered.

"Very well, indeed," the enchantress replied. As the ravens looked on in silence, Daria began her tale.

Long ago, in the forest surrounding the village of Vasaria, there lived a young maiden named Endora. She was raised by three crones in a small house deep in the heart of the woods. Endora's parents had died when she was still an infant, or so she had been told—she had no memory of them. The old women who had taken her in were the only true parents that she ever knew. They gave her shelter and provided for her needs, but they were strange in their ways. The crones were sisters who practiced the arts of magic and witchcraft. They were feared by some of the villagers, while others sought them out for their powers of clairvoyance and healing, or to cast away sinister spirits.

Over the years, the crones had instructed Endora in the Old Ways, teaching her the forgotten rituals and spells of the dark kingdom. Every day was devoted to the study and practice of the ancient arts. By the age of six, Endora could call forth birds and small animals from the forest and conjure a misty half-light to push back the darkness as she lay in bed at night. As she matured, so did her powers.

At the age of seventeen, the girl was fully attuned to the unseen world that surrounds us all and spellcasting had become second nature to her. And though she showed great promise, her youthful powers were meager in comparison to the magic of the crones, for their powers of conjuration and prophecy were unsurpassed. With little effort they could enter people's dreams, read their minds and even foresee their ultimate destiny.

Endora's adventure commenced on the first day of her eighteenth year. The day began as any other day in her young life. She woke with the rising sun, dressed quickly and hurried outside. The freshly blossoming plants held the morning dew in their leaves and the air was filled with the promise of new growth. As she walked through the woodlands, she neared the mountain road that led between the village and the Tower. She watched from the shadows as men trudged up the forest path carrying tools, timber and chiseled stones to complete their construction inside the King's castle upon the mountain summit.

The Tower loomed high above the forest pines and elms. Its dark spires jutted forth from the earth like the monstrous claws of some enormous beast trapped beneath the mountain. The castle walls had stood for several years, but the Tower's interior had not yet been completed. The King had found a new faith and had decreed that a place of worship be built within the castle to honor his newfound god. During his reign, pagan monuments that had stood for centuries were toppled. The Old Ways, it seemed, were soon to be forgotten.

Though Endora and her guardians lived within the King's realm, they did not abide by his decree. The crones worshipped an ancient sylvan deity known as Leshii, the Forest Lord. Leshii was said to be the avatar of the slumbering Dark Ones, an ancient brood of immortals who dwelt deep in the earth beneath the shadow of the mountain. These mysterious and powerful beings could be summoned forth by arcane rites, involving forbidden rituals and spells. According to the Old Ways, when a chosen maiden came of age, she was to unite with the Forest Lord in a pact to ensure the prosperity and success of the next generation. Endora had been chosen for this honor.

The crones had prepared Endora for the ritual, teaching her the ancient words and instructing her in the arcane rites of summoning. Endora's young heart held a mixture of fear and elation as she imagined her meeting with Leshii. She had never seen the Forest Lord before, but she had felt his presence whenever she ventured deep into the woods. This evening, she would know his desires.

As twilight descended, Endora set out on the path that led deep into the forgotten realms of the forest. The trail became narrow and overgrown with wayward roots as the woods grew denser. Overhead, the tangled mesh of vines and branches filtered the moonbeams to meager trickles of light, creating sparse patches of illumination along the path. As she passed beneath the forest canopy, the startling screech of an owl broke the calm of the sleeping woods. The eerie sound echoed through the trees, causing Endora to pause and scan her gloomy surroundings for wandering spirits or woodland nymphs, but there were none to be seen. Warily, she resumed her trek.

Far beyond the gnarled roots and thorny bramble, the woods retained their ancient magic. Here, deep in the wilds of the forest, the path became lush, carpeted with moss and lined with leaves of deep blue and vivid lavender. Endora realized that she could no longer hear the sounds of songbirds or the rhythmic croaking of frogs. Even the chirp and murmur of insects had ceased. The entire forest had fallen silent beneath an otherworldly and unsettling hush.

At last she came upon the clearing known as Raven's Hollow. In the midst of the grassy field, a circle of ancient stones had been set into the earth. Each boulder was crested with an age-worn inscription of a mystical symbol. Endora gathered dried twigs and branches to build a fire. As the flames illuminated the hollow, she undressed and stood naked amidst the ring of mossy stones. Lightly and with delicate reverence, Endora traced the faint outline of the mystic runes upon each stone. She began to chant in a soft cadence, repeating the ancient words and sacred vows, as she had been instructed.

The forest rumbled with thunderous footfalls that grew louder as they drew nearer. Beyond the treeline, there appeared a tall figure—a black shape against the dark shadows of the forest. The trees parted and a towering shadow stepped forth into the moonlit hollow. As it moved slowly into the clearing, pale moonlight fell upon its hulking body to bathe the figure in an auburn glow. The pagan creature resembled a man with a mane of long black hair, bearing a crown of horns like that of a great stag. Its lean, muscular body was naked but for a silken coat of dark fur covering its legs. The creature stepped forward on cloven feet, its long, whip-like tail encircling Endora like a serpent's embrace.

This was Leshii at long last, looming before her like a magnificent statue carved from solid obsidian. The ancient creature was even more beautiful and fierce than the crones had described. His eyes were burning embers of red and his lips parted to reveal gleaming white fangs.

His deep whisper shook the surrounding trees. "Thou hast summoned me?"

Endora stood speechless, staring in awe at the creature before her. At last she gathered the courage to utter a response. "Yes, my lord."

The Forest Lord's burning gaze washed over the girl's soft flesh. "Dost thou come here willingly, child?"

Endora bowed her head. "I do, my lord."

"Tell me thy wishes, child."

Endora strained to calm her pounding heart. "I seek your blessings, for myself and my kin."

"And what dost thou offer in return?"

"I offer to thee whatever thou desires of me."

Leshii smiled, pleased by her answer. "Then know this, child—wouldst thou surrender unto me, thy first born shall rise to rule this land, bound by blood to the dark gods of old." The creature's fiery stare grew brighter. "Wouldst thou seal this pact with thine own flesh?"

Endora gazed into the Forest King's eyes, falling spellbound beneath their piercing crimson glow. Softly, she whispered, "Yes."

"Then so be it," the Dark One's voice rumbled.

His black tail coiled around the girl's slender waist, drawing her close enough to taste the warmth of his breath. She felt the delicate caress of his clawed fingers upon her thighs. His slightest touch made her shudder with unknown ecstasy. She closed her eyes and threw her head back in rapture, surrendering her body to the pagan god. She felt weightless, as if she stood balanced upon the threshold of wakefulness and dreaming. The chill forest air had become warm within the dark creature's carnal embrace. Endora's legs trembled beneath her as she felt the pulsing weight of his body pressed against her own. Her heart pounding, her blood rushing fiercely through her veins, she became inflamed with desire. The Forest King lifted Endora from her feet and pressed his wet lips against hers. Taking her firmly in his muscular arms, the ancient beast carried her beyond the circle of stones and into the black woods, where, upon a bed of moss amongst the roots of a giant oak tree, they consummated their pact.

The lovers stirred as the sky began to lighten. Sitting up, Leshii drew a sharp claw across his chest. A rivulet of deep scarlet seeped slowly from the wound over his heart. He opened his other hand to reveal a small glass vial attached to a silken cord. Leshii pressed the vial to the wound on his chest, filling it with his heart's blood, then sealed it with a wooden stopper sculpted to resemble the head of a stag. The Forest King held Endora's gaze as he gently placed the amulet around her neck.

"The immortal blood that courses through my veins holds unearthly magic." The Dark One's commanding voice dropped to a husky whisper. "If used wisely, this shall help grant you your heart's desires."

Without another word, the ancient creature rose and lumbered away. His thunderous footfalls receded as he strode into the distance. Within moments he disappeared into the dark woods, becoming one with the shadows of the forest once more. As the dawn broke through the trees, Endora dressed herself and doused the embers of the ritual fire. Hastily, she returned home to tell the crones all that had transpired.

Shortly thereafter, the King's wife fell ill and was bedridden for several days. In a short time the Queen had become frail and weak. Her bright blue eyes became glassy and dull, her silken hair was frayed and her cheeks had sunken into darkened hollows. Each night she was plagued by the same nightmare of a monstrous figure lurking in the shadows of her room, watching her with burning red eyes. She claimed that she lay petrified by some dark spell as she watched the beast's black hand reach toward her. She felt its clawed fingers press against her chest and she gasped for breath as its icy grip closed around her heart.

Once, she awoke to see a demonic shadow hovering over her bed. The dark form disappeared when she screamed, vanishing into an ebon mist.

The Queen dreaded falling asleep, for there was no escape from her terrible nightmares. The unbearable torment drove her to madness until, at last, she sought a drastic end to her woe. She leapt to her death from the belltower. Her mangled body was found at the base of the keep and her blood stained the black rocks below.

The crones, in their dark wisdom, had foreseen the Queen's death and used the knowledge to set forth a plan. The old women sent Endora out to collect a mandrake root so they might concoct a spell to capture the King's grieving heart. Endora set out beneath the light of the full moon and returned with the first rays of dawn, carrying the plunder of her midnight harvest. As she entered the house, she was met by an eerie scene. Writhing shadows stretched across the walls as the three crones busied themselves stoking the fire beneath a large cauldron of bubbling brew.

One of the crones stepped forward, holding the amulet that Leshii had bestowed upon the girl. "Let us see what you have found, daughter," the old woman croaked.

Endora reached into the bag she carried and removed a pallid root resembling a wrinkled man. She held it forth and the hag let a single drop of the Dark One's blood spill upon it. The root wriggled and squirmed between Endora's fingers, as if trying to escape the girl's grasp. The crone's eyes filled with glee and a sinister smile crept across her face. The old woman snatched the writhing mandrake from the girl's hand and tossed the root into the blazing cauldron. A hellish squeal issued forth from the bubbling vat and the hag cackled at the sound.

The second crone read aloud from a tattered book filled with arcane symbols. Her raspy voice whispered ancient words whose meanings had long been forgotten by all but a few. The third hag plucked strange herbs and insects from earthen jars marked with mystical symbols etched into the hardened clay. She ground the ingredients to dust in a bowl carved of wormwood and spilled the contents into the vat, stirring it slowly.

Extracting a small portion of their concoction, the crones cast a spell of enchantment upon a black rose. The potion settled like dew into the velvety folds of the rose creating a perfect bloom that would never wither or die.

News of the Queen's death quickly spread through the kingdom, and the next day the villagers set forth to the Tower to attend the royal funeral. The Tower bell tolled every hour to mark the somber occasion. Crowds of mourners filled the castle grounds to pay their respects to their beloved monarch. By decree of the King, a priest of the new faith presided over the ceremony, which lasted into the early hours of evening.

As dusk settled, wandering minstrels played solemn ballads in tribute to their fallen Queen and torches were lit around the perimeter of the castle grounds. The flames wavered gently in the mild breeze, stirring a heady aroma of woodsmoke and herbs. In the distance, gypsy clans gathered around a great bonfire, drumming and singing to the spirits of the night. Endora stood alone, between the ornate stone columns that formed the castle gate, watching the gypsy ritual on the grounds below. High above, the moon and stars were just becoming visible, glittering faintly above the firelight.

The crones joined the ritual circle and the festive gypsy song slowly changed to a deep, droning chant. The voices merged with the low, steady drumming, creating a hypnotic rhythm that pulsed through the night.

After a short while, the King emerged from the Tower, as if summoned by the chanting call. He ventured out across the castle grounds alone, unescorted by his royal guards. An unseen force seemed to compel his actions as he ambled mindlessly toward the bonfire ritual. His hair and beard were long and tangled, flowing wildly in the wind, and a look of forlorn sadness filled his eyes. As he walked along the cobblestone path, he came upon Endora standing alone beneath the shadows of a gated arch.

The girl turned toward him, bowing her head submissively. "My King," she said in a soft voice, "I offer thee a simple gift to ease your grieving heart." She withdrew the black rose from a silken pouch and held it forth.

A slight smile formed on the King's sullen face. "What is thy name, child?"

"I am called Endora."

"Endora," he repeated. "Your sweet gift softens the bitter memory of this day. I shall not soon forget your token of kindness." He took hold of the black rose and was instantly captivated by its enchanting fragrance. As he stared into Endora's dark eyes, his passion stirred, and lustful desires roused deep within him. A fever swept over him like wildfire, heating the blood in his veins. The King closed his eyes to gather his senses, steadying himself against the marble gate. When he opened his eyes, Endora was no longer there and the distant chanting fell silent.

Later that night, as the King lay in bed, his mind flooded with images of the beautiful gypsy girl. He could think of nothing else as he drifted to sleep and into the realm of dreams.

He found himself wandering through the misty woodlands in the dead of night, roaming unknown wilds. Slowly, he followed a whispering voice carried by the wind until at last he came upon the fallen stones of an ancient castle. There, in the midst of the mossy ruins, Endora stood waiting. No longer the innocent girl he had met earlier, she now exuded a dark, provocative allure. Her right hand clutched a tall wooden staff, crowned with a crescent moon, while her left hand rested upon a human skull. She was draped in a gown of blood-red velvet that clung tightly to her ivory flesh. A mystic pentagram, symbol of the Old Ways, clasped a cape around her neck. Behind her, the sculpted likeness of a pagan beast was chiseled into the crumbling remnants of a stone wall.

Endora's eyes held an unearthly crimson glow that beckoned the King to come closer, but as he stepped toward her, a fearsome black shadow rose from the forest mists behind her. She gestured her hand toward the beast and the creature retreated back into the darkness from whence it came. She cast her mesmerizing gaze upon the King once more, drawing him closer still, then let her gown fall to stand naked before him. The shimmering glow of the moon's light caressed the soft, perfect curves of her body, giving her the appearance of a radiant goddess, the embodiment of mortal desire.

Without a word, Endora pulled the King to her, wrapping her arms around his waist, enclosing him in her seductive embrace. Her allure was irresistible and intoxicating, rendering the King her spellbound slave. He felt the warmth of her touch, tasted the sweetness of her lips and knew the pleasures of her submissive flesh. Again and again, she quenched his carnal desires, yet he greedily hungered for more.

As the new day dawned, the King awoke to discover another black rose on the table beside his bed. His chamber door was locked and the room was empty, save for a large raven, perched upon the window ledge. A small scroll was attached to the stem of the mysterious rose. As he unrolled the parchment, a thorn bit into his palm, drawing a droplet of his blood. The note contained a secret invitation from Endora, the dark beauty from his dreams. Her sweet voice whispered to him as he read her words, bidding him to meet her at the standing stone in the

woods near the village at midnight. The King smiled, enticed and intrigued by Endora's mysterious summons. He set the note down and turned his gaze toward the raven on the window ledge. The black bird spread its ebon wings and flew off toward the deep forest.

As evening came, Endora prepared for her rendezvous with the King. She bathed in the stream as the crones chanted prayers to the gods of old. Endora's body was anointed with the remainder of the enchanted potion, then she was dressed in a fine gown of dark linen. The girl's pale skin glistened in the moonlight and her dress took on a scarlet shimmer as it stretched across her shapely form. Her hair shone like satin and held the aroma of sweet lavender.

As midnight approached, Endora set out toward the village, seeking the monument that stood in a small clearing near the edge of town. The woods were strangely quiet and shrouded beneath a ghostly fog. Tall shadows stirred beyond the trees and seemed to follow her at a distance along the forest path. She quickened her pace, reaching her destination in a short time. As she surveyed the misty hollow, she found herself alone.

Entering the clearing, she came upon an enormous freestanding stone, its surface worn and etched with arcane symbols. Endora gazed upon the strange runes, silently reflecting upon the lost message they held. The night's stillness was interrupted by the sound of galloping hooves as the King approached on horseback. He dismounted and tethered his steed to the low branches of a nearby tree, then stepped dauntlessly toward the waiting girl. He wore a tunic of deep burgundy beneath a cloak of black velvet. His beard was neatly trimmed and his long hair was tied back, allowing Endora to admire the chiseled features of his face.

"Good evening, my King," Endora said, bowing her head

slightly. "It pleases me that you have come."

The King stepped closer, offering a rugged smile. "I shall please you in many ways this night." His eyes surveyed the hollow. "Why have you summoned me to meet you here, in this forsaken place?"

Endora leaned back against the ancient monument, stretching her arm across its weathered surface. "Do you know the tale of this stone?"

The King's eyes scanned the strange runes chiseled into the moss-covered boulder. "It is a remnant of the Old Ways," he replied, "inscribed with symbols of a forgotten time. Many of these pagan markers have been destroyed—toppled and broken by followers of the new faith. Why does this one remain standing?"

"Once there were three such monuments. They surrounded the mountain to mark the ancient boundaries of the Dark Ones. It is said that none of their brood can pass beyond the threshold of the standing stones. They are forever bound by an ancient pact to remain upon the mountain, or in the earth beneath it." She took a step back, beyond the marker and smiled playfully, as if daring him to cross the ancient barrier.

The King stepped across the threshold, saying, "No boundary can keep me from you." Taking Endora in his arms, he pulled her close, kissing her fiercely. Endora willingly gave herself to him, surrendering all.

Hours later, they lay in each other's embrace beneath a distant canopy of stars and moonlight. They spoke of many things, sharing their memories and dreams as they became lost in blissful reverie. Though their union was born of enchantment, the feelings they shared were true and sincere. The King stroked Endora's hair gently as she rested her head on his chest. She closed her eyes, reveling in the moment, and for the first time in her young life, she knew true happiness.

A rustling sound in the trees behind them alerted them to a shadow emerging from the misty forest. A large black wolf entered the clearing and crept slowly toward them. The King leapt to his feet, withdrawing his dagger and brandishing it before him. The wolf's eyes narrowed and changed to orbs of glowing red.

"No," Endora cried, rising to stand between them, halting their imminent clash.

"What manner of sorcery is this?" The King's voice rasped with rage and confusion.

Endora gazed deeply into the creature's crimson eyes, recognizing the spirit of Leshii within its molten stare. She turned to the King to warn him. "The guardian of the forest watches over me. He is protective of his children."

The dark creature loomed ominously behind the girl, returning the King's glowering stare with its own seething gaze.

Endora laid her hands upon the King's chest. Tears welled in her eyes as she pleaded, "Leave now, before you anger him further."

"Come," he said, taking hold of her hand. "Return with me to the castle. I shall care for you and make you my queen."

Though her heart yearned to be with him, she was bound by her pact to the Dark One. "I cannot," she whispered, kissing him tenderly. Endora's hand slipped from his grasp and she backed slowly away, abandoning the man who had swayed her heart, remaining instead in the custody of the black beast. "Farewell, my love," she said quietly.

The King returned to the Tower, to live out his days in loneliness. And though he never saw her again, Endora's sweet memory haunted his dreams each and every night. The King repented his sins, begging forgiveness for his lustful act, but his prayers would not save him, for the seed Endora carried, the seed of his own loins, would be the eventual seed of his own destruction.

When winter came, Endora gave birth to the King's bastard daughter. The hours of labor were difficult for the young woman, straining both her body and spirit. She lay in bed, shivering and breathless, weakened by the trying birth. The three sisters were busy muttering over a boiling cauldron. The fire in the hearth did little to dispel the aching cold that leeched through the stone walls and thatched roof, and the sickly sweet stench of dried herbs mixed with boiled roots and blood hung heavy in the fetid air.

Her newborn daughter was bundled in a clean blanket and tucked into a basket near the hearth. The child cooed softly as she wriggled to escape her wrappings. The old women turned from the fire to make their way back to Endora. One picked up the infant, while another held a cup of the vile brew, and the last carried a flint knife.

Laying the babe in Endora's arms, the first crone retrieved the cup and knife. She touched the cup to Endora's lips and urged her to drink a few drops of the ghastly potion. Then, placing the knife in Endora's hand, the old woman intoned, "What name dost thee give this child?"

"She shall be called Mara," Endora replied, gently touching the flat of blade to the child's forehead.

The crones busied themselves round the cauldron, adding a drop of the child's blood to the vat as they invoked the spirits of old. Their conjurations gave rise to eerie shadows that writhed and swayed across the walls and ceiling. Endora turned away from the infant and stared into the smoke that rose from the bubbling cauldron. Slowly, from the swirling fumes, a vision began to form, and a hush fell over the forest.

A beautiful young woman with long, ebony hair reclined upon a dark throne. A crown of black spikes rested upon her head and the silken tendrils of her ebon gown flowed from her sides like shadowy wings. Her ruby lips parted in a seductive smile, her teeth sharp and glistening red. Encircling the dais were dozens of wolves, and perched upon the throne were three ravens black as coal. Before her, spread across a cavernous room lined with columns of stone, were dead and dying men, women and children. The dark queen looked out over the carnage before her with cold, black eyes and smiled at the woe she had wrought.

As this vision cleared, Endora found the child strangely quiet in her arms, looking up at her with eyes black as night. The Forest King had promised that this child would rise to great power, but Endora now saw that this prophecy would only be fulfilled at the expense of mankind. Endora's vision forewarned of great suffering and destruction beneath the cruel reign of her daughter, Mara, several years hence. Tears streamed down Endora's face as she realized the grim outcome of her dark pact. The horror she had born unto the world would be the cause of endless torment for all humanity. She could not bear the thought. She gripped the knife and set the sharp tip over her daughter's tiny chest.

A shadow passed over Endora, startling her and causing her to look up, and as she did, she was captured by the petrifying gaze of the Forest King. The Dark One loomed over her, glaring down at her with eyes of burning hellfire. Endora screamed in rage and sobbed with remorse but her hand was stayed, her will no longer her own. Her hand trembled and pulled the blade away from the infant's pale flesh. With an anguished shriek, Endora plunged the knife downward into her own chest, twisting the blade deep into her heart.

The Dark One instructed the crones as to what to do with

the child. The old women agreed to bring the infant Mara before her father, the King, so that he could decide his daughter's fate. After the forest lord took his leave, the crones removed the dagger from Endora's chest, capturing her heart's blood in an amulet of silver. Endora's body was buried at the base of the standing stone, beyond the ancient threshold of the Dark Ones. It is said that her spirit can yet be seen there when the night mists rise, standing silently in the hollow, as if awaiting her lover's return.

Daria finished her story and paused as the wind rose to a mournful howl. "We have kept this tale secret for generations, fearing retribution from those who have suffered beneath the Tower's curse. Had the village elders learned that the magic of my ancestors was responsible for Mara's birth, we would have surely known their vengeful wrath."

Brom nodded. "I understand the risk you take by revealing this tale. I shall chronicle the legend, but shall tell no one else." His pale eyes conveyed a look of sincere gratitude and his stern tone softened. "I am in your debt."

"No, Lord Brom. The wisdom you have gained this night shall help us all."

Brom looked down at the mystic circle where the candles burned low. "Your halo of protection wanes."

Daria smiled. "As does yours."

The Tower Lord turned to see the night sky brightening with the rising dawn.

"Farewell, Lord Brom," Daria whispered.

Brom gave the enchantress a parting nod then quickly took his leave, vanishing into the depths of the forest. As he made his way back toward the black spires that rose in the distance, the ravens in the surrounding trees took flight, following the dark lord to the looming citadel that cast its bleak shadow over the land.

The Forgotten

JOSEPH VARGO

Spirits of the dead haunt these shadowed halls and grounds. Their hollow whispers echo in the night whilst their phantoms wander the graveyard and stir from their crypts below the Tower. I have always known of such things. When I was a boy, my uncle spun stories of ghostly specters and the restless dead, claiming that he had in fact witnessed one such spirit with his own eyes. He told me his tale many times, swearing on his oath that his words were true. Though many years have passed, his words remain etched in my memory and his tale haunts me still.

Never being one to believe in ghosts, witches or other such lore, I considered myself a skeptic on such things—that is, until the night I found myself hopelessly lost in the wooded countryside of Ebonshire.

I had somehow veered off the main road, and after a while the cobblestones beneath my feet dwindled to a stony path that snaked its way through an ever increasing density of trees. The forest eventually whittled the path to a sparse dirt trail that had nearly been engulfed by a blanket of fallen leaves. To each side of the path moss clung to boulders, and twisting vines entangled themselves among the gnarled trees. The lush foliage of the dark woods had the effect of rendering the surrounding landscape as the setting of a wicked fairy tale. A feeling of uneasiness crept over me as I imagined myself being spied upon by the various sylvan spirits and creatures of folklore that were said to inhabit the deepest shadows of the forest.

Good sense would have dictated that I turn back and retrace my steps to the last village that I had passed, as it was approaching evening and I had no torch, but curiosity prodded me to discover where this trail might lead and the adventurous heart in me bade me to proceed in my current direction. The sun had started to set and the meager light that penetrated the thick growth of trees gradually began to fade. I slowed my pace and stumbled aimlessly until my eyes adjusted to the near-pitch darkness of the forest. I proceeded cautiously and as quietly as I could, fearful that I might draw the unwanted attention of some nocturnal predator.

After some time, I spied a faint blue light in the distance, and using it to guide me like a beacon to its source, I advanced warily forward to investigate. An evening fog had begun to creep between the trees, and as I drew closer to the mysterious glow, I beheld an unexpected sight in the mist-shrouded woods. A young woman draped in a sheer white gown appeared to be wandering in the dead of night. She drifted slowly through the mist toward a stone marker which stood at a crooked angle amidst a thick growth of vines. The tattered tendrils of her silken gown wavered and floated in the still night air as if held aloft by some undetected breeze. The pale blue glow seemed to radiate from her body and gown. As she drew near the marker, I could discern the details of what appeared to be a tombstone overgrown with a mesh of tangled vines. I watched in silence as the girl tenderly caressed the marker, running her fingers lightly over the twisted vines and across the weathered stone. At last she fell to her knees and hung her head, covering her face in her hands.

I stood frozen in place, mesmerized by this eerie vision,

until at last I regained my composure and summoned the courage to approach her. I had advanced to within a few yards of the girl when a twig snapped beneath my foot. The sound of the breaking branch startled the girl, who at once drew back, lifting her head to gaze in my direction. Her flesh held a deathly pallor, and her eyes were completely drained of color. My mind whirled as I tried to make sense of the macabre sight before me. Her soulless eyes opened wide and I stood transfixed by her ghastly stare, then without so much as a whisper, the girl vanished into the mist.

In the vast expanse of a lifetime, one is invariably likely to be subjected to strange and unexplainable events, but none more unsettling than the vision I had just witnessed. I stepped forward to examine the neglected marker. I extended a hand to verify that it was real and not merely a fabrication of moonlight and shadow playing tricks on my mind. The stone was solid, and the cracked and weathered surface of the aged monument was deathly cold to the touch. I shuddered as I wondered whose grave this might be and why it stood neglected in this forsaken place. Further conjecture led me to wonder who this mournful spirit was and what significance this grave held for her. The absolute silence of the woods added to my uneasiness, and I resumed my trek through the forest, leaving the forlorn grave and its spectral mourner far behind.

After a length of time, I came upon a crossroads, but no signpost stood to mark the way. This time I chose the more traveled road and continued my march at a quickened pace. Eventually, I came upon a small village and made my way to the tavern. After a brief introduction to the few occupants inside, I warmed my hands at the hearth then took a seat at the bar and proceeded to relate the night's events to the bartender.

The old man let me recount my tale without interruption, then he gave me a wry smile and said, "You've seen the phantom maiden at the grave of the forgotten."

"Who was she?" I asked.

"It was long ago," the bartender replied, "so long ago that no one remembers her name, but her tale is one of tragedy and despair, and stories such as these have a way of enduring the years." The old man paused for a moment to re-light his pipe, then he began his tale. "As it is told, she was once a beautiful lass in the full bloom of womanhood and she was deeply in love with a young lad from the neighboring village. They desired only each other and wanted nothing more than to live out their days together. The lad asked the girl's father for her hand in marriage, but his proposal was refused in light of a brighter prospect. Another suitor offered wealth and land, and the girl's father granted his blessing for their marriage. The date was set for the wedding, but on the eve of their betrothal, the girl's husband-to-be was found murdered, his throat slit ear to ear.

"The girl's lover was arrested for the murder of his rival suitor. At first he denied the deed, but after some time he succumbed to the tortures of his inquisitors and confessed to the murder, as well as being in league with dark powers. He was hanged and his body was buried in that forsaken place beyond the unmarked crossroads so that his spirit would not be able to find its way back to town.

"The lass was stricken with grief and lapsed into a listless state. Her father's words lent no solace to her sorrow and physicians could offer no remedy for her condition. Eventually the girl found comfort in death's sweet embrace."

The bartender ended his tale and said no more.

After a long and somewhat uncomfortable silence, I

asked, "So she visits his grave, still? The grave of this rogue who murdered for her?"

The bartender shook his head and said, "You do not yet understand what your own eyes have witnessed. The fact that his spirit was not present while hers yet wanders the night, can mean only one thing." His voice lowered to a hoarse whisper as he confided, "The tragic truth of the matter is that beneath that weathered and vine-encrusted gravestone lies the body of an innocent man. His spirit knows eternal rest, while the true murderer is cursed to haunt that forsaken place, ridden with guilt and remorse, returning each night to the forgotten grave of her one true love."

Countless generations have lived and fallen before my eyes, and yet I see no end to my crusade here. I feel myself slipping, as if the parapet were crumbling away beneath my feet. I cling to the remaining stones as do the gargoyles that line the Tower, but my strength fades with each setting sun. And as my resolve weakens, so does my grasp upon the final vestiges of my humanity.

Dark Desire

JOSEPH IORILLO AND JOSEPH VARGO

The mysteries of the Dark Tower are vast and elusive, spanning countless centuries of tragedy and woe. The sinister secrets buried within its ancient walls have haunted and terrified all who have dared to dwell beneath its grim shadow, leading many a soul to doom and damnation. Legends say that its black curse dates back to the Antediluvian age, stretching back through the annals of time to the dawn of man. Though many tales of the Tower's origins exist, the thresholds between fact and fable have been obscured by aeons of superstition and lore.

Throughout my years as lord of the keep, I have toiled steadfastly in my attempt to piece together the castle's fragmented history. The elders of Vasaria have revealed their secrets to me, offering all they know of the sinister fortress that looms ominously above their village, but their knowledge spans little more than a century before becoming clouded by myth. The treasury of ancient tomes and crumbling scrolls filling the Tower's library holds the archives of the kings of old, but their pages were penned in numerous long-forgotten languages. Many of these archaic documents were deciphered and translated by the Baron, who chronicled his findings in a series of journals during his own lonely vigil in the Tower.

Although the Baron compiled his legacy of research with the hopes of enlightening his successor, much of his wisdom eludes me. His journals are filled with cryptic revelations, open to wide interpretation, whose exact meanings are impossible to grasp. Within these tomes, strange and erratic thoughts intertwine. Enigmatic prophecies and occult diagrams share the pages with arcane mysticism and blasphemous philosophy. I have struggled in my quest to untangle the web of chaotic, interwoven thoughts that the Baron felt compelled to relate. In the midst of his fanatical scribings, however, I have on occasion discovered fully translated chronicles of the region's shadowy past, documented without interruption.

One such journal recounted a tragic saga from a distant age. On the first few pages, the Baron's familiar, jagged handwriting spoke to me across the years, describing an ancient scroll that he had found concealed in the base of a statue within the Tower's chapel. Penned in Enochian runes, the mysterious scroll was aeons older than any other document he had discovered in the library. Where it had come from and how it came to be hidden here was unknown, even to him. He described the manuscript as the confession of an immortal being—an angel who had inhabited the Earth during the dynasty of the Watchers. On the pages that followed, the Baron presented his translation of the scroll.

By the Lord's decree, I descended from the eternal kingdom of Heaven to the earthly domain of man. Here I stand vigil, watching over the mortal realm, a witness to mankind's evolution. I have silently observed their growth and endeavors with great curiosity. Across the breadth of several millennia, they slowly developed from savage, instinctive beasts to creatures of mild intellect and reason. Through the ages, their petty quests for dominion of their world gave rise to widespread civilizations. As a race, they are a primitive lot and their flaws are many, yet they are not without virtue. Though they strive to overcome their mortal limitations, they are often toppled by ignorant, selfish actions. Even so, there are some who have impressed me with their strengths and selfless deeds.

The men are callous and headstrong, but they possess an indomitable determination and courage that compels them to reach far beyond the boundaries of their mortal abilities. In their women I have found an innocence and charm, an endearing tenderness and grace unmatched by my master's most magnificent creations. Over the fleeting centuries, there have been some among them who have roused my heart, stirring the fires of passion within me, captivating me with their earthly beauty and gentleness. But alas, they are fragile creatures and their lifespan is a mere fraction of my own. Through the ages, they were all lost. I watched each of them blossom to the fullness of life, only to wither and die like a frail rose in winter.

Mortality haunts these beings like a relentless demon, allowing them only a brief span of happiness upon this earthly plane. Often I have felt that there are some mortals who do not deserve this fate, who deserve instead to take their place next to us, the immortal ones, never fearing the ravages of time, never knowing pain, weakness or death.

My heart fills with sorrow as I write the name Iliana...

Many generations ago, during the dawning of man's civilization, I watched over a village from the foothills of our mountain summit and witnessed the rise in power of Valkonour, a fierce warrior who defended his realm from marauders and barbarians. A wise and stern ruler, Valkonour was both beloved and feared by his people. Among the humble, meek villagers he strode with a kingly air, and I watched as he spent years building from stone a fortress home for himself and his young bride.

Shortly after the birth of his first child, Valkonour saw his wife murdered by an enemy assassin, struck down by a poisoned arrow meant for him. And though sadness settled like a cloud over Valkonour's life for some time, the cloud dissipated as his daughter Iliana grew. The solemn, dark-haired girl with skin as pale as moonlight was a gentle counterpoint to her harsh, unrelenting father, and as she blossomed into womanhood, her angelic beauty attracted many suitors. Most were driven away by her father, who found them unworthy, and some were repelled by Iliana's shyness and reclusive nature. She spent much time alone in the woods, and as I watched her over the years I sensed a deep yearning within her heart for something she could not find among the lowly stablehands, farmers and brutish warriors in the village. Often I would see her as the sun set, gazing off toward the horizon, a look of melancholic desperation on her face, as if she felt that she would never find happiness or love.

It was on one such evening that I chose to ease Iliana's sorrow. The sadness in her dark eyes seemed to call out to me with a bewitching power, and I heedlessly answered their plea. In the guise of raven, I took flight to Valkonour's fortress and alighted on a tree near Iliana. She watched me with great interest and curiosity, her face filled with kindness and the childlike wonder of her youth. I spread my wings and beckoned her with my mind, drawing her to me with my stare. She stepped closer and instinctively reached out her finger, coaxing me to fly to her, but instead I took flight toward the forest. Landing on the branch of another tree, I looked back and called out to her with the raven's raucous cry. Without hesitation, Iliana followed.

The sun slipped further below the horizon and the woods grew murky with threatening shadows, yet as I soared from tree to tree, Iliana maintained her pursuit. She picked her way over rocks and gnarled roots until the woods ended in a small clearing deep in the heart of the forest. Arriving ahead of her, I assumed my earthly form. When she emerged from the forest, a handsome young man with raven-black hair awaited her in the clearing. Despite my smile and peaceful demeanor, however, Iliana stood wary and kept a cautious distance from me.

"Do not be afraid," I said. "I mean you no harm."

"Who are you?"

"Someone who has watched thee for many years—a kindred spirit who knows thy heart, and the longing that resides within it."

Iliana took a step backward, pausing on the verge of fleeing. I made no move toward her but held out my hands to show her I posed no threat. "I have watched thee blossom into a beautiful young woman, full of kindness and honor," I told her, "but I also sense a sad emptiness within. You have shown tenderness and mercy to others, yet happiness eludes you, and you seek something that you cannot define, something you do not see in the mortal world that surrounds you."

Iliana's eyes widened. "How can you know this?"

"Thy plight is plain to see."

"What do you want of me?" Iliana's sweet voice was barely a whisper.

"I wish only to share a few moments in time with thee, to know thy gentle company and ease thy loneliness." I took a step forward and gazed upon her longingly, my eyes betraying the desire in my heart.

"I must go," Iliana said, so softly that her voice was no louder than the rustle of a leaf in a tree. She stepped backward into the shadows, though her eyes still gazed at me with curiosity and fascination.

"Visit this place again," I said, "and you shall find me here."

In the ensuing days, Iliana returned to me several times, and her initial fear of me waned and vanished entirely, replaced by a sense of wonderment. One evening, as a gentle rain fell, I lifted a hand and watched as her sweet face lit up in amazement, for the rain upon us ceased, though it continued to fall outside of the invisible circle in which we stood.

"Thy powers are those of a god," she said, "or perhaps the sorcery of a demon." Her tone was playful, but she then seemed to become lost in somber thought.

"What ails thee, lovely Iliana?"

"My father's superstitions," she replied. "I have kept our meetings a treasured secret, for I know they would strike terror in my father's soul. He has travelled throughout these lands and seen much unexplainable horror. He believes that dark forces always besiege us, whether we know it or not."

"I am no demon," I said to her, softly stroking the smooth arc of her cheek. "I am a Watcher. My kind has overseen man's time on earth from the beginning. We offer our guidance to those who seek it, but we do not interfere in the affairs of mortals. Your destiny is yours alone to fulfill."

Iliana stared at me in bewilderment. "You watch us suffer, yet do nothing to end our woe?"

I said nothing in my defense.

Iliana's eyes filled with melancholy. "Did you watch my own mother perish?"

I could not lie to her. "Alas, I did," I said quietly, revealing the bitter truth.

"As you will no doubt watch me perish one day." There were notes of disappointment and sadness in her voice.

Again, I said nothing.

"I must go," she whispered, withdrawing reluctantly into the rain and hurrying back through the woods.

In the foothills above the village, I watched the dim lights of hearthfires in the crude abodes miles below me while two of my elder brethren, Arius and Mordala, stood silently beside me, their wings folded about them like shadowy cloaks.

"Thy affection for this girl has not gone unnoticed," Arius said. "Thy emotions seem to have made thee forget the history of our kind. When we involve ourselves with man, the consequences are inevitably tragic. Thou knowest our laws. It is forbidden to mix our blood with theirs. Recall the fate of the banished ones who took mortal women as mates and guided them in the ways of magic. Their offspring inherited our abilities, yet their powers were corrupted to become dark and sordid."

"Only sorrow will come of thy love." Mordala's voice held a dire tone. "Thine own wisdom should tell thee that her life is but a short breath while yours will span aeons. Thou art older than this mountain, my brother, thou art older than this world. Thou shalt continue to live long after her bones have turned to dust. She is trapped in time while thou art not."

"It does not have to be so," I whispered as I turned away.

Alas, my feelings for Iliana blinded me to the wisdom of my brethren. Heedless of the consequences, I foolishly ignored their warnings in pursuit of my own desires. The next evening Iliana and I stood on the banks of the lake near the village, and I took hold of her hand for the first time.

"Your touch is vibrant and warm," she said, "like the coal from a fire."

The bottomless pools of her young eyes were more lovely than anything I had seen in the countless millennia of my life, and as I stared deeply into them Mordala's words rang in my head like a mournful tolling bell. Her life was indeed but a short breath, and soon she would pass from this earth while I would still be holding vigil here, haunted by the memory of this perfect girl.

"To be with thee forever," she said, seemingly to herself, "is all my heart desires. Yet I know this is a foolish dream, for I am condemned to be a mere mortal."

"Thy life is no condemnation," I said. "Thou wilt know thy share of joy and pleasure."

Her fingers intertwined with mine and again a sadness crept into her eyes. "But not enough," she whispered.

I drew her near and she clasped her arms around me. Sleek, black wings manifested behind me, rising from my back to encircle her. Her eyes conveyed a look of wonder as I held her in my angelic embrace. I looked to the turbulent storm clouds in the heavens and carried her aloft into the dark skies above. Together we ascended silently, flying over the slopes of the mountain, the cool air and the clouds rushing by us. We continued to fly upward, and in moments we landed on the rough-hewn precipice of the mountain, the wind howling around us like a chorus of lost souls. Her gossamer gown billowing in the wind, Iliana clung to me desperately, and I could feel the insistent pounding of her heart.

The breathtaking, majestic view of the lands below us held her transfixed, and she whispered a single word. "Beautiful."

I lifted her delicate chin with my finger and gazed into her eyes once again. "Do you truly wish to leave your mortal life behind to be with me eternally?"

"Yes," she whispered, "yes."

"Then it shall be so," I said, raising my hand before her face.

Iliana stood in silent anticipation as she watched raven's claws emerge from my fingertips. I raked the talons across my wrist, slicing my flesh open wide. A trail of crimson ran from the wound to glisten darkly in the moonlight. Raising my arm, I held my wrist to her trembling lips.

"Drink deeply," I told her softly. "Thy life shall be strengthened by my blood and thou wilt become as I am."

Iliana lowered her mouth to my flesh and sucked slowly from my wrist, consuming the sanguine gift I willingly offered. A warm trickle of blood escaped her lips and ran down my arm and Iliana hungrily lapped the crimson stream with her tongue. She shut her eyes, her expression becoming one of unearthly, sensual serenity. I turned my head to the raging heavens and chanted the ancient words of the Seraphim aloud, completing the forbidden ritual.

I pressed my lips against hers and whispered, "My blood shall make thee immortal. Never shalt thou age, never shalt thou know the pain and struggle of mortal man." I stroked her smooth, alabaster cheek as her head fell back in ecstasy. I felt a surge of tender triumph in my heart, for this wondrous, flawless creature with her goddess-like beauty would be preserved forever, an immortal rose.

The power of my life-force within her kept her in a slumbering trance, and I spread my wings and carried her back down to the valley and the woods near her village. I laid her gently on the forest floor and bestowed a kiss upon her forehead. An unearthly vibrancy and strength seemed to emanate from her even in sleep. Neither age nor illness could harm her now; only fire or the purest, sanctified silver blade could ever still her perfect heart.

In the following days, our meetings in the forest had a passionate joy that will haunt me forever. With a childlike innocence and enthusiasm, Iliana proudly demonstrated her newfound powers. Her eyes shut in deep concentration, she would extend her hand into the air and suddenly a thunderous fluttering of wings would be heard in the trees around us as flocks of ravens arrived and perched upon the branches, watching her keenly as if awaiting to do her bidding.

Once, near the stream within the forest, she held out her

delicate hand and the rushing water changed direction. Her eyes filled with glorious delight. I soared across the water and joined her on the far bank, and she folded her arms about me and I felt the seething touch of her lips on my own. I felt as if our life together was just beginning.

Among my own kind in the foothills overlooking her village, however, I met with the chastising gazes of Mordala and Arius.

"Thou hast ignored our warnings," Arius said. "Thou hast become blinded by selfish human desires."

I responded angrily to the accusation. "I could not bear to watch the girl's innocent soul wither and die when I possess the power to bestow her with immortal life."

Mordala stepped close to me. "Thy gift is one of damnation, for the power thou hast given her hast corrupted her innocence. This will not end as you wish it to."

Beyond the disappointment in their words, I sensed a pall of dread.

In silence, we watched the village below us as night descended. Blazing torches surrounded Valkonour's fortress. "The villagers live in fear," Arius said. "Wolves have been found slain in the forest."

"So it begins," Mordala said softly.

My time with Iliana became less frequent from then on. Some evenings I did not see her at all, though I sensed her in the forest. Mordala's words echoed in my head many times when I heard the frightened howl of wolves in the distance. Once I came upon the carcass of a freshly killed stag at the edge of the creek, its throat torn viciously open, its body drained of all blood. A trail of human footprints led away from the scene and Iliana's scent lingered in the air.

For the first time, I began to doubt the wisdom of my gift

to her. These misgivings turned to dread when I witnessed her savage actions with my own eyes. I spied her in the distance one evening, stalking one of the woodland wolves as the animal drank from the lake at the far end of the valley. Clad in a sheer black gown, she crept through the grass like a graceful spider and sprang upon the wolf, tearing its neck open with her hands. She drank in the spray of warm blood with a wild desperation, draining the creature's life as she quenched her ferocious thirst. The taste of my immortal blood had awakened the primal beast within her.

"It will not stop with the animals of the forests," Arius told me some nights later as the full moon glowed balefully above us. "Of all man's flaws, greed is perhaps his most deadly. Man never ceases to want more than he deserves and to take more than his due. He is always a slave to his hunger... a hunger that never abates but always grows in power. The gift you have given this girl has only roused her bloodlust, awakening some dark, unquenchable desire within her."

Though they condemned my reckless actions, my brethren could not intervene, for I had bestowed Iliana with her newfound powers, and I alone could revoke them. At sunset on the eve of the new moon, I watched from a distance as Iliana led a young man toward the entrance to the forest. The young man, so obviously bewitched by her beauty, followed breathlessly, his eyes wide with lust. The brief flare of betrayal I felt in my heart was replaced by rising horror as I noticed the savage, predatory glare in Iliana's once lovely eyes. She ran her fingers down the young man's neck and chest and pressed herself close to him, stoking the flames of desire within him. She held his face in her hands as if to kiss him tenderly but she bared her sharp teeth instead.

"No!" I bellowed, my voice ringing out through the forest like thunder.

Startled, she released her grip on the young man and he stumbled backward, falling to the ground.

I leapt into the fray and stood between Iliana and her intended victim.

Iliana's eyes flashed with rage. "He is mine," she hissed in a voice I barely recognized. She raised her arms in a conjuring motion and the ravens of the forest answered her summons. In an instant, the black birds swarmed the skies above her, filling the air with a terrifying chorus of croaks and screeches.

The young man watched in astonishment as the ravens flocked to the surrounding trees, their eyes glistening like fading embers as they reflected the setting sun. "Sorceress," he whispered, retreating further from Iliana. Without another word, he scrambled away and sprinted back toward the village.

Iliana turned her furious gaze upon me. "He was mine!" she screamed in outrage. "His blood was mine!"

The ferocity in her tone was unfamiliar to me. "What has become of you, Iliana?"

"I thirst!" Iliana's shrill cry echoed through the trees, silencing the shrieking ravens. "And my desires shall not be denied!"

She bared her teeth and lunged at me in a vicious rage, but I raised my hand, whispering the ancient words in the sacred tongue, words that still possessed their timeless power and which even now shook the branches on the trees around us like a strong breeze. Iliana fell to the ground, trembling. Her face paled, confusion and sorrow filling her eyes. The fierce power that had taken hold of her had dissipated.

"I am sorry," I said.

"You have taken my strength from me." Iliana's voice had returned to her natural, soft tone.

"I have restored your humanity, Iliana." It was true. She

was no longer the dark immortal creature I had witnessed mere moments ago. She had once more become the innocent, delicate mortal that had captured my heart. Though her soul had been spared, my eyes clouded with tears, for I knew that many countless centuries from now I would still overlook these lands while my beloved Iliana would be little more than dust and memories. She pulled away from me and I could feel my heart breaking.

"Forgive me," she whispered tearfully, turning and running back to the village through the dim of twilight.

The next evening, Arius and Mordala stood with me in the foothills as I watched the village below. "Do you now see the tragic price of interfering with the destiny of mortals?" Arius asked.

I did not reply.

"Thou hast shamed thyself through these transgressions," Mordala said sadly. "There shall be harsh consequences for thy actions."

"Do as thou wilt," I replied solemnly, conceding my guilt and remorse. "My own feelings punish me far more than your judgments, my brother."

"Thy punishment shall not be delivered by us, nor shall it end here," Arius said. His tone was kind but grim. "Thou must see the end of what thou hast wrought." He gazed downward at the village, where a sudden burst of flame from Valkonour's courtyard caught my eye. Arius laid his hand upon me and we suddenly transformed into ravens. I followed as he soared down to the village, and the two of us alighted on a tree inside the walls of Valkonour's stronghold.

A crowd had gathered around an unlit pyre, a large roughly hewn pole rising from the pile of dry logs and thatch. Two of Valkonour's servants had lit large torches and stood on either side of the pyre.

I listened to the ragged, angry chanting of the villagers, chanting that called for the death of Valkonour's sorceress daughter. Dread overcame me as I watched the stern appearance of Valkonour himself, followed by two more of his servants, who escorted a bound and struggling Iliana. She wept and begged her father to release her, but Valkonour did not so much as look back at his only child.

Valkonour walked to the young man I had seen with Iliana several nights ago. The crowd quieted as Valkonour asked the man to repeat his account of being seduced and nearly killed by his daughter. In a shaky voice, the young man related his story truthfully. Valkonour's hand trembled on the hilt of his sheathed broadsword, but he merely nodded. Several more villagers stepped forward with tales of savaged livestock and sightings of Iliana preying upon the forest wolves.

For the first time, Valkonour faced his daughter.

"Father, please release me," she begged. "How can you do this to your own flesh and blood?"

"I too have seen you steal away in the dead of night," he said softly, "and I have seen you return stained in blood. A spirit of evil has seduced you." His voice had become ragged and threatened to break. "This spirit must be driven out to rescue your soul from damnation." He nodded curtly to the men holding his daughter, and they forcefully brought her onto the pyre and tied her to the pole. Iliana thrashed and shrieked, and I longed to fly to her, but Arius' glare was upon me, restraining me. I could not move.

Valkonour gently stroked his daughter's silken hair one final time, then with the resolve of a battle-hardened warrior he stepped back from the pyre and fell to one knee, his head bowed. He recited a prayer of spiritual deliverance from evil. Many of the villagers likewise bowed their heads and echoed his words. Iliana's unceasing shrieks and sobs drowned out their voices. Her face was a mask of the purest terror. Valkonour nodded to the servants bearing the lit torches, and they walked to the pyre as Iliana's screams became more frantic and terrified. In moments the logs blazed and the flames writhed across Iliana's body like glowing snakes, and I watched as her once flawless skin reddened, becoming darker and darker until it was as charred as a burned field. Her shrieks had become animalistic wails, and her moist, desperate eyes found mine and stared into my soul with a pleading that I will never forget. After reaching an agonizing, deafening pitch, the screaming stopped, though the flames burned many hours into the night.

Arius took flight but I remained near my Iliana, and here forever shall I remain, my penance the unceasing memory of those eyes, pleading to me for a mercy I could not give. My own weakness corrupted her innocence and brought about her demise, and I shall bear the guilt of my sins eternally. Valkonour said a spirit of evil had seduced his beloved daughter, and as the ages pass I often ponder his words, wondering if the mortal brute had more wisdom than I.

The Watcher's tragic story lingered in my mind long after I had finished reading it. As I reflected upon his sorrowful confession, his tale mingled with memories of my own lost love, striking a familiar chord. Like the tormented Watcher angel, I too had vainly attempted to share my immortal life with the woman I cherished, and I too had been responsible for her demise.

'Tis said that a wise man learns from the sins of the past, gleaning the wisdom to never repeat his transgressions. Even so, my sins cannot be undone and my heart beats heavily with guilt. And though it seems I am destined to never know forgiveness for my deeds, I continue to endure the long, trying years as I serve my penance in this accursed Tower with the hopes of someday finding deliverance for my own anguished soul, and salvation for the one I have damned.

Restless spirits yet linger here,

wandering these unhallowed corridors.

Their mortal mission unfulfilled,

they implore the living

to help them end their plight,

seeking redemption for their sins

and exacting vengeance

upon those who have wronged them.

Each phantom has some tale to tell,

some lost wisdom to share,

some macabre secret to impart

from beyond the grave.

Their whispered words hold the power

to shatter the ties that bind them here,

for the key to their ultimate salvation

lies in the revelation of truth.

Death Grip

Joseph Vargo

Thunder rumbled throughout the darkened heavens as howling winds delivered violent torrents of rain to pelt the ancient stones of the Tower. Jagged streaks of lightning ripped across the midnight sky, illuminating the fierce legion of gargoyles perched along the lofty ledges of the sinister keep. Each furious thunderstrike revealed more and more of the ominous guardians that kept silent vigil from the Tower's shadowy heights. Winged monstrosities with the features of men and beasts lined the castle battlements like a hoard of hell-spawned demons, awaiting their infernal master's commands. The stone sentinels peered downward defiantly, scowling and bearing fangs with gleeful menace as the storm raged around them. Their clawed fingers and talons clutched the black stone, and as the downpour intensified, streams of ruddy water gushed from their gaping mouths. The tumultuous storm seemed to imbue the nightmarish creatures with unearthly life.

In the castle below, Brom stood in the sanctity of the keep's entrance hall with Leonidas, envoy of the village elders, and waited for the storm to pass. Among their various duties, the council of elders acted as emissaries between the people of Vasaria and the Tower Lord, keeping Brom appraised of all current affairs. Leonidas had travelled to the Tower often throughout the years and had come to know Lord Brom well. On this night, however, a sense of unease gripped the old man's heart.

The fury of the storm had caused Leonidas' horse to bolt and break free of its tether, sending it galloping down the mountain path, back toward the village. Now, he was stranded at the castle in the midst of night and the dark lord's looming presence did little to calm the old man's worries. Leonidas nervously surveyed his dismal surroundings. Torches set in sconces around the room's perimeter cast a dim yellow glow that faded to darkness before reaching the chamber's gloom-shrouded heights. Sporadic bursts of lightning allowed brief glimpses of the monstrous gargoyles that loomed overhead. With each blinding flash, the macabre guardians seemed to emerge further from their shadowy roosts, stretching downward through the cobwebs, leering hungrily.

Brom sensed the old man's discomfort. "They are merely stone," he said quietly, "nothing more." The Tower Lord's mirthless tone offered little consolation.

"Yes," Leonidas said. "But through the years I have discovered that things are seldom what they seem here."

A slight smile formed on Brom's ashen face. "I have never known you to be fearful of this place, old friend."

"Then I have hidden my feelings well. I am not as superstitious as most, but I have witnessed a lifetime of darkness and sorrow here—enough to know that the Tower is haunted by more than one devil."

Brom's black eyes caught the reflection of the flickering torches. "There are those who would count me among the demons that dwell here."

"Pay them no heed, my lord." The old man's voice conveyed sincere concern. "Their simple minds cannot fathom the truth. The elders know of your plight here. We know of your sacrifices and tribulations. You are in our prayers each night. All of Vasaria is in your debt."

Another thunderstrike drew Brom's attention back to the gargoyles that loomed overhead. His nocturnal vision penetrated the gloom to see the sinister creatures lurking beyond the veil of shadows. "I have often wondered why such sculptures adorn the keep. Are they beasts of local myth?"

Leonidas drew his cloak tight around his shoulders to stave off the night's damp chill. "There are countless tales of their origins and purpose. Many of the statues outside the Tower have their own names and stories in village legends. There is Os Devora—the bone eater, Diavolul—the devil bat, Tibor—the winged wolf, and Drakosom—the dragon fiend. These are but a few of the ones I recall. It is said that on moonless nights, the statues come alive and leave their towering perches in search of prey. They prowl the dark woods, stalking the shadows, searching the forest with eyes of burning hellfire. Villagers warn their children of the dangers that lurk in the darkness and say prayers to keep them safe from harm. In a child's mind, it is not difficult to believe that such stories are true."

Brom continued to peer into the shadows overhead, his eyes scanning the faces of the grotesques. "Who would sculpt such monsters?"

"According to the legends, they were not molded by human hands," Leonidas replied. "It is said that the Dark Queen used her powers to change the Tower, transforming the very stones to fit her twisted vision. Her sorcery created a foreboding realm of nightmares befitting her wicked nature."

Brom glanced toward the darkened archway that led deeper into the Tower. "Yet, some places remained untouched by her vile magic. The graveyard within the castle parapet holds statues of angels and saints, as does the chapel."

"Yes," Leonidas affirmed, "Mara's powers hold no sway

over sanctified ground." The elder's gaze returned to the shadows overhead. A thunderstrike illuminated the ferocious creatures once more. "Whatever their origins, these ancient guardians yet serve as potent wards against intruders."

"True," Brom said. "There is one, however, that seems strangely out of place. It sits upon a pedestal on the staircase landing near the Tower balcony—a horned demon clutching a human skull. Each time I pass it, the statue's face seems different. Its countenance appears to shift from expressions of fierce savagery to mournful woe, to mocking laughter."

"Ah, yes," the old man murmured, nodding.

"You know of it?"

"I have never seen it, but I have heard its tale many times."

"It is a tale I should like to hear," Brom said, stepping closer.

"Very well." The elder cleared his throat. "It began long ago, during the reign of the Dark Queen. As you know, Mara was once a mortal—the bastard daughter of an ancient king who ruled these lands. Though her father provided for her needs, he showed her little affection. Isolated and neglected, Mara felt entitled to more. In her loneliness, she found solace in a dark tempter who swayed her young heart and led her down the path of shadows. She sacrificed everything she knew of her mortal life for the promise of power and everlasting beauty. It is told that when Mara inherited her sinister powers, the demon that seduced her into darkness appeared to her in the guise of a court jester—the living image of one of the castle sculptures. The demon bestowed his curse upon Mara by tainting her blood with his own, making her part of the Fallen Ones' immortal bloodline.

"The statue you speak of once resided in the Tower's grand

hall, beside the king's throne. Though Mara surrounded herself with grim and sordid works of art, this lone sculpture plagued her. She was haunted by it. Legends claim it holds powerful magic. Some say it reminded her of her own mortality in the devil's grasp. Others believe that the statue holds the trapped souls of her victims and that their ghostly cries tormented her. Whatever the truth may be, she had the monstrous sculpture removed from her sight and placed on the Tower landing, where it remains to this day.

"All who have gazed upon its face describe it differently. To some, it bears a ghastly countenance, ominous and terrifying, while to others it portrays looks of sorrow and sinister glee. It is as if the stone itself shifts to taunt each viewer."

Brom stood silently for a long moment, staring into the darkness above him as he contemplated the old man's words. Yet another secret of the Tower had been revealed, and once more, the explanation had left him with even more unanswered questions.

The sounds of the storm relented. Brom walked toward the massive twin doors at the keep's entrance. Taking hold of the heavy iron latches, he pulled them effortlessly toward him and the great doors creaked open. Thunder rumbled in the distance, but the downpour had subsided to a mild rain. As the Tower Lord stepped outside, Leonidas followed close behind.

Brom turned to the old man. "I shall fetch your horse and bring him back."

"No." Leonidas shook his head. "I am not so old that I cannot walk down a hill." He rested a strong hand upon Brom's shoulder and smiled reassuringly. "I shall be fine." The elder strode down the Tower steps and dauntlessly headed back along the forest path toward the village.

Brom watched Leonidas disappear into the dark woods

then returned to the Tower, bolting the heavy doors behind him. As he turned to make his way back through the entrance hall, a strange sight held him rapt. A vaporous form appeared near the foot of the grand staircase at the far end of the chamber. Brom stood motionless and silent as the spectral mist manifested into a tall, stately man draped in the regalia of the ancient kings. Long, dark hair framed the spirit's pallid face and a jeweled crown rested upon its head. The phantom cast its deathly gaze in the Tower Lord's direction and Brom stepped slowly forward. Without a word, the spectral king ascended the grand staircase, its long robes and cape flowing in the air behind it.

Brom quickly made his way across the hall and followed the majestic spirit up the staircase, keeping a discreet distance between them. The phantom trudged relentlessly onward, slowly climbing the winding stairs to the keep's towering heights. As the specter neared the balcony landing, it turned to meet Brom's gaze. The ghost's ashen face conveyed a look of dire sadness, then its mouth gaped open wide and its flesh withered away. Within seconds, the regal spirit had decayed to a cadaverous visage. The frightful wraith drifted into the shadows of the balcony landing, fading from sight. As Brom rounded the staircase corner, he discovered the phantom was gone. Instead he was met by the ghastly demon statue perched upon its stone pedestal. The hellish beast loomed menacingly as it guarded the skull clasped in its monstrous grip.

Brom stood before the macabre sculpture, silently scrutinizing its intricate details as he pondered why the spectral king had led him here. Brom reached a bone-white hand toward the perfectly sculpted death's head in the gargoyle's grasp but paused before touching it, his fingertips hovering above the grim memento. A mournful howl rose on the wind and whistled through the balcony gate behind the stone demon. The ominous wail grew louder, filling the air with an eerie cry, like a shriek from the grave warning Brom to turn back. Ignoring the ghostly omen, Brom laid his hand upon the skull. A bitter chill swept up his arm and instantly spread throughout his entire body. Brom closed his eyes for a brief moment and when he opened them, he found himself in another place and time.

He stood in the center of the Tower's grand hall amidst a sea of human carnage. Scores of dead bodies adorned in strange costumes and masks lay heaped around him, scattered throughout the dimly lit chamber. Swarms of ravens feasted upon the corpses, greedily tearing flesh from bone. The ravens' cries echoed in the hall, drowning out all other sounds.

As Brom surveyed the grisly spectacle that surrounded him, his attention was directed to the dais at the far end of the chamber. A court jester dressed in a bloodstained costume of black and white sat on the king's throne and a young woman, draped in a sleek ebon gown, stood before him. The jester held a golden staff bearing the king's severed head, contorted and frozen in a deathly grimace. Brom recognized the dead king's face as the face of the ghost on the staircase.

The jester rose and descended the stone dais, a maniacal smile upon his painted lips. The sinister harlequin removed the crown from the king's head and dropped the staff to the floor. He stepped toward the woman and raised the crown high, then placed it upon her head. As Brom watched the macabre scene unfold, he realized that he was witnessing the unholy coronation of Mara, the Dark Queen.

The jester pulled Mara close and kissed her softly. He whispered in her ear then lowered his mouth to her throat. His black lips drew back to reveal long fangs, jagged and razor-sharp, like those of a wolf. The jester's teeth pierced the girl's young flesh, sinking deep into her neck. Mara shuddered and writhed, caught between rapture and pain, then collapsed in the harlequin's arms.

Unable to interfere, Brom watched helplessly as the horrific scene played out before his eyes. The jester carried Mara's lifeless body to the top of the dais, gently placing her in her father's throne overlooking the great hall. Brom shifted his gaze to a pedestal beside the dais, where a familiar gargoyle sat perched. It was the same grim statue that rested on the balcony landing, yet something was different. Its clawed hands were empty, clutching nothing other than the stone base beneath it.

The harlequin picked up the staff bearing the king's severed head and tore the grisly trophy free. Stepping toward the devilish gargoyle, the jester held the king's head before the statue's hands. The stone demon's lifeless eyes filled with a seething red glow. Its monstrous hands opened to clutch the head in their stone grasp, then the beast's clawed fingers tightened around it, digging deep into the sockets of the dead king's eyes. The severed head burst into flames, becoming engulfed in a halo of hellfire. The unearthly flames consumed the king's flesh until all that remained in the gargoyle's deathly grip was a smoldering skull.

The diabolic jester took a step back and as he did, his form grew dark and obscure, becoming a mass of writhing shadows. The black cloud rose and churned like a storm until, at last, it settled into the shape of a towering, winged beast. The creature's head resembled a monstrous bat, its eyes ablaze with a crimson glow. Its shimmering flesh was black and smooth, as if it had been sculpted from solid ebony. A long, serpentine tail swept behind it as it stepped toward the dais. Brom recognized the dark creature as the demon that had visited him one night long ago in the castle graveyard.

Mara roused from her slumber, awakening to find herself seated in the bloodstained throne. As her black eyes surveyed the gloom-shrouded chamber, a ghastly smile formed upon her blood-red lips. The shadow beast loomed before her amidst the morbid terrain of corpses and feasting ravens. The demon spread its massive wings and rose to the heights of the hall then vanished into a dark swirling mist.

The ravens fell silent and faded from sight. The dead bodies that covered the floor began to wither and decay, rotting to skeletons before Brom's eyes, as if years were passing in mere seconds. Mara remained seated in the throne, seemingly frozen in time, as cobwebs and dust formed upon the gargoyle at her side. A ghostly mist began to stir at the base of the statue, eventually rising to take human form. At last it manifested itself into the spirit of the dead king. Bathed in an unearthly glow, the specter stood motionless beside the fiendish gargoyle. The stone demon's face twisted to a mocking howl and the phantom's lifeless eyes locked upon Mara in a solemn stare. A look of horror swept across the Dark Queen's face and she turned away, unable to bear the sight of her father's ghost.

As the years passed, the king's spirit returned again and again, hovering beside Mara's throne, haunting her for her murderous deeds. Each time his vengeful wraith appeared, the demonic statue's expression twisted to one of fierce scorn. The Dark Queen was plagued by the taunting gargoyle and the fearsome skull in its grasp, but her magic held no sway over the accursed monument. Powerless to destroy the statue, Mara ordered her minions to remove the cursed sculpture from her sight, commanding them to hoist it to the Tower landing where her father often stood, surveying his kingdom from the balcony window.

The dreamlike vision grew dim and Brom returned to his own thoughts, his hand still resting upon the skull. He took a step back from the morbid statue, keeping his eyes locked upon the gargoyle's chiseled face. For the first time the stone beast seemed to convey a look of contentment, as if its anguish had finally subsided. Brom mused that the balcony was indeed a fitting resting place for the fallen king who built the Tower high upon the mountain summit. Taking firm hold of the statue's base, he turned the heavy sculpture in its place, twisting it around to face the balcony window, directing the skull to gaze down upon the kingdom below.

Brom turned to leave but paused at the edge of the stairs. "I shall chronicle your tale for all to know," he said aloud, his deep voice echoing in the hollow stairwell. He awaited a response, but his declaration to the long-dead king was met with empty silence. Perhaps, Brom thought, the spirit had fulfilled his ghostly mission, freeing him from his earthly bonds. Perhaps, Brom hoped, his tormented soul was finally at rest.

Bloodlines

Joseph Vargo

As night's starless cloak settled over Vasaria, a lone raven spread its ebon wings, taking leave of its perch among the monstrous stone guardians that kept eternal vigil along the battlements of the Dark Tower. The black bird plunged from the ancient spire, then glided on the rising wind, sailing high above the path that snaked through the forest of thorns and vines as it descended toward the village. A blazing light shone from the heart of the town, sending a fiery beacon to catch the dark creature's eye. The bird circled the village several times, then flew back toward the ominous citadel that loomed high on the mountaintop. There, amidst the nightmarish gargoyles that lined the castle's heights, Brom awaited the raven's return.

The Tower Lord stood atop the battlements, his black cape billowing in the wind behind him as he looked out over his domain. Winged hellhounds clung to the ledges on either side of him, their fierce claws clutching the ancient stone, their fanged mouths gaping wide. On most nights, Brom ascended to the parapet to stand watch over the distant village, but on nights such as this, when the moon shone full, he focused his gaze on the gated arch beside the tower road, hopeful to catch sight of the spirit that wandered there.

The flutter of wings drew Brom's attention to the sky above him and his eyes followed the returning raven as it descended from the black of night. The onyx bird came to roost upon the sculpted monstrosity at his master's side, digging its talons into the shoulder of the hellish beast. Setting its black eyes on Brom, the grim bird cawed hoarsely, as if to inform the Tower Lord of all it had seen. Brom's gaze penetrated the raven's cold stare, allowing him to peer deep into the creature's thoughts. In his mind's eye, Brom soared high above the forest landscape. In Vasaria far beneath him, a bonfire burned in the center of town, sending a pillar of sparks and smoke into the night. The townspeople stood gathered round the blaze, their heads humbly bowed in silent prayer. In the midst of the fire, a skeletal figure lay engulfed in swirling flames.

Brom returned to his own mind, contemplating the macabre ritual he had witnessed through the eyes of his winged emissary. At times such as these, when the plague carried pestilence and death from village to village, those who died of illness were not buried in the local graveyard. Their bodies were sanctified and cremated on funeral pyres. Brom wondered whose body lay on the blazing pyre, but he did not dwell on the thought, for he knew that on the morrow one of the village elders would come to the Tower to inform him of the tragic details.

Brom cast his gaze once more toward the ruined arch beside the road. Beyond the gated threshold of the Tower's domain, the ground began to stir. A white mist slowly rose from the earth and began to assume a ghostly form. The vaporous figure became more and more defined until at last it manifested itself as a woman shrouded in white. The specter slowly glided toward the central arch of the gate but faded from sight before it reached the marble ruins.

The raven cried out again, alerting its master that someone was approaching the Tower. Detecting the visitor's scent on the wind, Brom shifted his attention toward the forest, intently scanning the treeline for signs of movement. Though the canopy of twisted woodlands obscured his view, Brom discerned the faint rustling of footfalls upon leaves. Curious, yet wary of his visitor's intent, the Tower Lord returned to the castle to await his guest.

Far below, a cloaked figure emerged from the forest path and quickly made its way toward the Dark Tower, disappearing beneath the keep's looming shadow. The great doors of the ancient castle stood slightly ajar, offering a narrow gap between them. Though the perils of trespassing upon the Dark Lord's domain were known by all, the figure moved heedlessly forward, silently slipping through the opening and into the entrance hall.

As the intruder crept forth, the muffled sound of his footsteps echoed throughout the immense room. Twin staircases curved around the far end of the chamber, stretching upward to meet at a balcony overlooking the hall. A shadowed archway beneath the balcony led deeper into the Dark Lord's forbidden realm. Dim moonlight shone down through tall windows, coming to rest upon a blood-red design emblazoned on the center of the dusty marble floor. A raven descended from the darkness above and landed upon the crimson sigil, locking its black eyes on the intruder. The bird relinquished a shrill croak, then fluttered away, disappearing into the shadows of the arch beneath the staircase. Without hesitation, the dark figure followed the bird further into the castle.

The trespasser descended a flight of age-worn steps and proceeded along a musty, gloom-shrouded corridor. Rounding a corner at the end of the narrow stone passage, he paused between two doorways. To his left, skeletal angels supported a stone archway, framing a heavy wooden door upon which three cryptic words had been carved. To his right, a twin doorway stood open, revealing a dimly lit chapel beyond its threshold.

A solitary candle burned in a red votive glass above the chapel's altar, casting a crimson glow upon the ancient sanctum. The intruder quietly entered the room, turning his cowled head from side to side as he walked between a series of stained glass windows depicting sinister scenes of cruelty and woe. At last he came to stand before a stone relief portraying a conflict between angels and demons. He gazed upon the sculpture for a long moment, reverently admiring it, as if the piece held deep significance for him.

Suddenly a bitter chill, as frigid and inescapable as death itself, crept over the room. The intruder turned to face the open doorway but found no one there. Turning back, he was startled to see a man in black robes now standing behind him, watching from the darkness beyond the candle's reach. The watcher's face was concealed in shadows, but there could be no doubt as to his identity. This was the dark master of the Tower, Lord Brom.

"Only fools trespass where angels fear to tread." Brom's voice sent deep echoes throughout the chapel. "I do not welcome strangers."

"I am no stranger to this place," the intruder said. "Years ago, you offered me the sanctuary of this chapel."

The cloaked figure threw back his hood, revealing a face that seemed distantly familiar to Brom. The Tower Lord cast a scrutinizing gaze upon his uninvited visitor, recognizing him as a boy from the village. It had been nearly six years since their destinies had crossed, but Brom remembered him well. He had rescued the boy from the forest wolves one winter's night and brought him to stay in the Tower's sanctum until daybreak. The years had been kind to the child, for the boy had grown into a sturdy young man.

"So I did," Brom said, "but that was long ago." His voice

lost some of its cold menace. "I did not ask you your name when last we met."

"Nor I yours," the young man said, "though I discovered it soon after I left here. I am called Lorand."

"Why have you returned here after all these years, unannounced and uninvited?"

"I beg your forgiveness, my lord, but there was no other way. The elders would not grant me a formal audience with you. It is forbidden for anyone outside their ranks to venture here. I came here at great risk, without their permission, seeking only a brief moment of your time."

"Why?"

"To share a tale with you and ask you one question."

Brom remained motionless among the shadows. "Such a mission hardly seems worthy of the risk. What compels such recklessness?"

"I am deeply troubled—plagued with the desire to know the truth about something that happened long ago, and I fear only you can resolve my dilemma."

"How so?"

"My tale concerns you, Lord Brom," the boy said, then hesitated, as if gathering the courage to continue, "and the fate of a woman who once lived in Vasaria. I have heard the story many times throughout my life, for it is often told to warn children of the perils that lie in wait here."

"Then speak it, if you would have me hear it." Brom's words conveyed slight discomfort.

Lorand drew a deep breath then began his tale. "Long ago, in the village of Vasaria, there lived a maiden, innocent and beautiful as an untouched rose. One night, beneath the light of the full moon, she ventured deep into the woods along the mountain path. She came upon the Tower Lord as he stalked the forest in search of human prey, for as it is told, the demon quenched his thirst upon the blood of mortals. Fear pounded in her heart as his black shadow fell upon her. She tried to run, but his freezing gaze held her in her place. She raised her rosary cross to ward off the fiend, but the dark lord unleashed his black sorcery, uttering an incantation that caused her to lower the sacred symbol. He wrapped his black wings around her, suffocating her in his diabolic embrace. Ignoring her cries of mercy and heedless of her beauty, he killed her and drank her blood to quench his monstrous thirst. After the demon bled her dry, his ravens devoured her flesh, picking her bones clean. She was never seen in Vasaria again."

Upon finishing his story, Lorand stood silent, his eyes fixed upon the Tower Lord.

"And what is your question?" Brom grumbled.

"I ask you, is this tale true?"

Brom stepped from the shadows, his eyes reflecting the candle's red glow. "I rescued you from the wolves and yet you still think me a monster? Did you discover nothing about the truth of my nature during your last visit? Did you not doubt the legend of my sinister allegiance? Did you not question the tales of the villagers when they spoke of my vile deeds and unholy powers? Did you not suspect they were merely dark fables?"

Lorand stood firm beneath the Dark Lord's ridicule. "As I said, I had heard the story many times. I did not believe it, for I could not fathom that the man who had shown me mercy and kindness when I was in need could ever be such a villainous fiend. Yet earlier this day I learned something that has set my mind to wonder. My heart will not rest until I discover the truth."

"Why does this weigh so heavily upon you?"

"My father died this day," Lorand said quietly. "On his deathbed, he revealed a secret he had kept for many years. He told me that though he had been proud to call me son, I was not his own flesh and blood. He raised me as his own, in the absence of my true parents. He clutched my hand and with his dying breath he uttered one final secret." Lorand's voice grew weak. "The woman in the tale, the one you murdered long ago—she was my mother."

Brom circled the black altar, stepping back into the shadows. "Tell me, boy, what was her name—this lost beauty of your tale, the woman you claim as your mother?"

Lorand glared at the figure that stood in the darkness. "Rianna," he said.

The word echoed around the chapel, then a hush befell the room. Brom felt his spirit collapse, as if a crushing weight had fallen upon him. A rekindled sadness took hold of his heart and a thousand thoughts flooded his mind.

"Have you nothing to say?" Lorand asked. "I accuse you of the murder of an innocent woman, yet you do not deny the deed."

Brom stared deeply into the boy's eyes, seeing the reflection of his own sorrow and pain. "I cannot deny the truth," he whispered, "just as I cannot escape the bitter consequences of my act. Only now do I fully realize their tragic extent." He stepped from the darkness into the halo of crimson light. "Life's path is a twisting journey. Things are seldom as simple as they seem."

Brom turned to face the chiseled relief depicting the struggle between the forces of light and darkness. "Years ago, I ventured to this place to smite the evil that dwelled here and rid Vasaria of the fearsome lord that reigned over these lands. I dared to challenge the Baron of the Tower, never suspecting that ending his life would seal my own eternal fate. With his death, I inherited his grim legacy and curse. I took his place as the lord of the Dark Tower and have since spent my days in solitude, searching for a way to vanquish the darkness that yet lurks here.

"I have undertaken a dire mission to guard the Tower. My penance includes enduring pain and temptations beyond mortal comprehension. The Tower Lord before me fell to madness, but he chronicled his cryptic wisdom for me to decipher and learn from. Before he came here, the Baron was a holy man. Like me, he followed a righteous path until, at last, his destiny brought him to this place. He vanquished the Dark Queen and her horde, but he did so at the cost of his own humanity.

"I have since uncovered the sinister bloodline that binds each master of the Tower. The legends trace the lineage back to the demon queen Lilith and her brood of fallen angels. The blood bestows mortals with unearthly powers, but wielding such power has a costly toll. For if it is not used with great wisdom and restraint, the power corrupts men's hearts. Those who surrender to their desires surrender their souls to eternal darkness and damnation."

Lorand stepped toward Brom, stopping within arm's reach of the Tower Lord. "Since the day I returned from the Tower, I have defended you." The boy's words contained a harsh ring. "When the townspeople spoke of your savage nature, I reminded them that you were our protector. I told them your wrath was reserved only for the wicked and that all who met their deaths at your hand were deserving of their fates. But now I have discovered a grim truth. You are no better than the others of your tainted line."

Brom's eyes glistened with rage, then settled once more

into a look of sadness. "I confess my guilt freely. But know this—though I took her life, I had little choice." He turned from Lorand and grumbled, "Come with me."

The Dark Lord led the boy through a door at the rear of the chapel into the graveyard behind the Tower. Twisting trees and ancient monuments rose from a murky sea of fog, creating an eerily tranquil landscape throughout the burial ground. Time-worn headstones stood at crooked angles to mark long-forgotten graves, and statues of angels kept silent watch over the dead. An angelic lector stood upon a marble pedestal and read from a chiseled book, while another winged statue held its arms outward in a gesture of peaceful, beatific welcome. Two more sculpted angels stood grim guard on either side of a mausoleum gate adorned by an ornate cross of black iron. Amidst the neglected tombstones, cracked and overgrown with vines, one grave was well cared for. Brom led Lorand to stand before the grave. Though most gravestones were weathered beyond recognition, the inscription on this marker was plain to read. The headstone bore a solitary name—Rianna.

"Here lies her body," Brom said. "The tale surrounding her death is more fable that truth. Allow me to cast light on the shadows."

Brom stared off toward the distant moon and for a moment seemed lost in reminiscence.

"I knew your mother long ago, before I bore this dark curse. She was, as your story described, a vision of beauty beyond compare. In all my life, my eyes have never beheld a woman so fair." Brom paused as he lingered upon the memory.

"After I became the Tower Lord, she ventured here of her own will to comfort me and ease my loneliness. I foolishly succumbed to my own heart's desires and attempted to share my life and legacy with her, but it was not to be. The blood ritual led to her ruin. A sinister force took hold of her and Mara was reborn. Little did I know that the Dark Queen could use others as a passage into the mortal realm.

"The spirit within your mother's body was no longer her own. She was possessed by an ancient evil. I ended her life to spare her soul from damnation. Her death was ultimately my greatest gift to her—one of spiritual salvation. I do not expect you to fully understand the sacrifice I made, nor the pain that yet burdens my heart. I suffered dearly for my deeds. I now know I must remain alone with my grief—such is my fate, as surely as it was the Baron's before me." He stepped before Rianna's headstone, laying his bone-white hand upon it. "I have sworn a vow on her grave," he said solemnly. "I will not falter again."

Brom turned to face Lorand and withdrew a longsword from beneath his cloak. He held the gleaming blade outward to catch the shimmer of moonlight. "This sword was given to me by the Baron. Its steel was not forged in any earthly fire, nor was it tempered by the hand of any mortal. It was bestowed upon ancient crusaders by a heavenly warrior, to aid them in their sacred mission. It is the only weapon that can slay those of my bloodline." Brom's eyes lingered upon Rianna's gravestone once more. "It is the same blade that drove the demon from your mother's heart."

Lorand stood silent, keeping his eyes locked upon the Tower Lord.

"No words can express the depths of my sorrow." Brom offered the hilt of the sword to the boy. "If you seek vengeance, then take this blade and end my life." Brom reached his free hand into a pocket of his robe, then held forth a rosary with crimson beads. "If, however, you can find a shred of forgiveness within you, then take this. It belonged to your mother." Brom added quietly, "A gift from your father."

Lorand's hand hesitated between the two choices as his mind wrestled with his decision. "I came here only to learn the truth, and I have heard it. You have suffered long with this guilt, and I believe your regret is sincere. I cannot doom humanity for your one reckless deed. I grant you my forgiveness."

He took the rosary from Brom's grasp, clutching the blood-red beads in his fist. A single tear fell from the boy's eye, landing upon his mother's grave.

Brom laid his hand upon Lorand's shoulder, ushering him back toward the Tower. "We must all face darkness in our lives. There may soon come a time when you are called upon to serve our cause."

"I am many years from becoming an elder."

"You are wise beyond your years," Brom said. "You are destined to be of avail."

Brom escorted the boy back through the keep to the arched gate that stood before the Tower.

Before taking his leave, Lorand turned to Brom one final time. "You have told me much of my mother, Lord Brom. Yet I know nothing of my true father. Can you tell me anything of him?"

Brom searched his heart for the words, then said at last, "Only that you have made him proud."

Lorand gazed back at the Tower, its black spires reaching up toward the moon. "The last time I left here, you made me promise to never look back upon this place."

The hint of a smile formed on Brom's face. "Yet here you stand. Somehow your path continues to lead you to the Tower. I feel your destiny may yet lie here."

"Then I shall welcome it," he said. "Farewell, Lord Brom."

The boy returned along the mountain path toward

the village.

"Farewell, my son," Brom whispered. As Brom stood at the gate and watched the boy vanish into the shadows of the forest, a soft voice rose upon the wind.

"I longed to tell you of him," the voice echoed gently in the night.

Brom turned his gaze toward the marble ruins that stood beside the road. There, beneath the central arch, stood a beautiful woman shrouded in white. "Rianna," Brom whispered.

The spectral beauty glided forward, speaking softly, "The elders decreed that no one should know of the boy's dark heritage—for the child's own sake and yours as well. They meant only to protect him. The infant was switched with a stillborn babe and raised in the home of another family. No one suspected the truth."

Brom's eyes remained fixed upon the phantom of his lost love, longing to hold her in his arms once more. "The elders were right to keep this secret," he said. "It would be too dangerous to reveal that the boy is my son. If Mara's followers learned the truth of his heritage, they would come for him and try to use him against me. I cannot allow this to happen. They must never know of him."

Rianna's ghostly hand reached out to caress Brom's face, but he felt only a chill upon his cheek where her fingers came to rest.

"A storm is looming," she said. "Beware, my love."

With that, Rianna's spirit faded from sight, leaving Brom alone in the darkness once more.

The Crimson Circle

JOSEPH VARGO

A low, mournful wail whistled along the ancient stones of the Tower, winding through the shadowed halls to reach the innermost confines of the keep. Deep in his library sanctum, Brom sat within a dim halo of candlelight, surrounded by shelves of time-worn books and scrolls. The ghostly sound penetrated the chamber, rousing the Tower Lord from his thoughts as he studied one of the Baron's journals. Rising from his chair, Brom closed the leather-bound tome, setting it down on the large oaken table before him, then proceeded to investigate the noise.

Following the howling call, Brom hastened along a series of narrow, cobweb-strewn corridors and ascended the staircase to the entrance hall. The eerie cry resounded in the great circular chamber, sending murmurs echoing in all directions. Brom peered into the shadows above, where hunched gargoyles leered and scowled from their perches overlooking the hall. Monstrous forms of winged beasts and nightmarish demons clung to the cornices surrounding the vaulted ceiling. Brom had become quite familiar with each of the Tower's stone guardians over the years and though their distorted faces portrayed looks of menace and woe, their silent company strangely eased his solitude.

Spying no sign of movement among the grotesques, Brom turned his gaze toward the Tower's entrance, where the wind hissed through a narrow opening between the keep's massive doors. Stepping cautiously closer, he squinted through the gap into the dawning day. Drifts of snow pressed against the castle walls, surrounding the black stones with tall, icy slopes. The mountain road between the village and the Tower was no longer visible—lost beneath a blanket of ivory white. It was the eve of the winter solstice, and the harsh winds and snow had severed his ties to the outside world, completely isolating him in the Tower.

Brom pulled the immense doors tightly closed and the howl subsided. Sliding the heavy bolt across the latch, he retraced his steps back to the library, content with the knowledge that the keep was secure. He knew that no one from the village would travel to the Tower until the spring thaw. The solstice marked the beginning of his winter exile.

As Brom walked back along the hollow corridors, another matter now filled his thoughts. The unrelenting hunger that he fought to suppress weighed heavily upon him. His unquenchable thirst for blood never subsided. The burning need was ever-present deep within him, like a fire that could never be extinguished. Brom did not hunt for nourishment, as did the others of his kind. The village elders brought him the blood of slaughtered livestock to appease his savage thirst. He had several casks stored in reserve for the winter, but he would need to ration them to last until the mountain road thawed.

Though Brom could go without blood for long periods of time, there were consequences for depriving his macabre thirst. The starving need would drive him to the brink of madness, as it did the Baron, and he feared that the madness would weaken his moral resolve, eventually leading him to succumb to his dark desires once again. Brom's heart filled with dread at the thought of sharing the Baron's tragic fate—becoming a monstrous fiend, a vile creature of darkness, unable to resist his own sinister urges.

The Baron had once been a holy and righteous man—a

martyr who had selflessly sacrificed his humanity to save mankind from the rise of the Dark Queen. He endured great suffering in his struggle to resist the savage hungers that welled within him as he sought to discover a path to salvation. And though he spent countless years searching for an answer to save his tainted soul from the darkness that gripped him, in the end, even he could not evade his own inevitable downfall. But in his search for deliverance, the Baron had discovered many of the secrets that the Tower held, chronicling his findings in his journals. If salvation existed, Brom knew he would have to study the Baron's research in an attempt to glean knowledge from his mad writings. The Tower Lord quickened his pace back to the library to busy his mind piecing together the fragmented wisdom of his predecessor.

Returning to his inner sanctum, Brom now noticed a scroll resting on his reading table. The rolled parchment had not been there when he left, of this he was certain. He stood silent, scanning the chamber for traces of an intruder, but could detect nothing else out of place. Though no other living souls dwelled in the Tower, Brom knew that he was never truly alone here. Throughout the years he had borne witness to a host of ancient spirits wandering the halls of the keep. Some were forever trapped within the castle's walls, while others were merely visitors from realms beyond the earthly domain. It seemed that one such spirit had left this scroll for him to find, perhaps to impart some message to him.

Brom carefully unrolled the heavily yellowed parchment to discover a tale written in an ancient flourish. He ran his fingertips across the brittle manuscript, and felt a static sensation, as if the page were empowered with a vitality all its own. As he began to read the mysterious scroll, his mind filled with images of times long ago.

High atop a mountain summit where the earth met the sky, a brood of dark creatures dwelt and wallowed in lewd revelry. Though they possessed knowledge and powers far beyond the comprehension of mortals, they were wicked and without virtue. These were the Fallen Ones, the rebellious outcasts from the eternal kingdom, banished to the earthly realm.

During the midst of a tumultuous storm, the thunderclouds that loomed above the mountain parted and three angels descended from the heavens upon silvery wings. They carried with them swords of radiant steel and were adorned in suits of gleaming armor. The heavenly warriors set down upon the summit and came to stand before the throne of the brood queen, Lilith, to deliver a divine proclamation unto her.

"We have come for you, Lilith," the first angel spoke, his deep voice resounding like thunder. "By the Lord's decree, you shall return with us to the realm of Eden."

"I have no desire to serve man," the brood queen hissed, leaning back in her throne defiantly. "I am content to remain here among the others who have been forsaken by our almighty father. We no longer wish to succumb to His will."

A dark creature with wings as black as ebony stepped forward to stand between his queen and the trio of warrior angels. "If you have come as the deliverers of the Almighty's vengeful wrath, to punish or destroy his creations, then know that we stand united. We will give our lives defending our queen." The creature's eyes filled with a burning red glow. "If you declare battle against us, your blood will stain this mountain along with our own."

The second angel spoke. "We will raise no sword against our brethren, but we cannot allow you free reign over this world. The earthly realm is destined for the Lord's mortal children, mankind. You shall not corrupt their innocence. If you are truly content with your existence here, then so be it. We shall set forth boundaries to mark the borders of your domain and we shall grant you sanctuary as long as you remain here, upon this summit."

Lilith's eyes narrowed as she surveyed her realm. "And what if these lowly mortals venture beyond the thresholds you have set?"

The third angel spoke. "The Lord has bestowed his mortal children with free will. Those who wander into your domain of their own accord have chosen their own fate. But should you dare venture beyond the set boundaries, or force your will upon those outside your domain, the consequences will be beyond reckoning. The wrath of the Almighty is swift and inescapable. You and your lot will meet your ultimate end. Your existence will cease and you will return to the dust from whence you came."

And so the pact was struck. Three standing stones were erected, surrounding the base of the mountain. Each marker was etched with the names of the three angelic guardians, inscribed in the ancient language of runes. And though none of the brood set forth beyond the standing stones, in time, mankind ventured into their dark domain. The brood came to be known as the Dark Ones by the mortals who worshipped them. But these newfound gods were wicked and cruel, and took pleasure in the torment of mankind. Throughout the centuries, human blood was spilled and sacrifices were offered to appease their sinister hungers. In time, mortals grew to fear and shun them, and fled from the region, and the Dark Ones retreated to the caverns deep within the mountain, seeking refuge in the shadows of the earth.

Aeons later, the legend of the Dark Queen and her brood was all but forgotten, and mankind returned to inhabit the surrounding lands. A castle was erected upon the mountaintop, and a Christian chapel was constructed within its walls. Men gathered in their place of worship and the sounds of their prayers penetrated the earth, awakening the slumbering gods of old. The ancient creatures opened their watchful eyes once again, illuminating the darkness with their

crimson glow. The time of the awakening had come, and the Dark
Ones rose once more, as if summoned forth by a beckoning call.

Brom finished reading the tale and laid the scroll down on the table where he had found it. If the legend was true, the Tower itself had been built upon the unholy domain of the Dark Ones. He recalled the standing stone that loomed in the clearing beside the forest path on the outskirts of Vasaria. Its age-worn surface held strange runic inscriptions, half-covered with moss and vines. He realized that he had crossed the ancient threshold of his own free will when he first came to the Tower.

Intrigued and mystified by the tale on the scroll, Brom spent the remainder of the day searching the library for more accounts of the legend, but could find no other record of it. When he returned to his reading table he noticed that the scroll was no longer where he had left it. It had vanished just as mysteriously as it had appeared, but something new had been left in its place. A ring of ancient symbols was drawn in the dust of the table where the scroll had been. Though he could not decipher the meaning of the unknown symbols, the arcane design seemed vaguely familiar to him. After a moment of reflection, he recalled where he had seen it before.

As the sun began to set, Brom stood in the chapel. The waning rays of daylight illuminated the western windows, sending a circle of crimson light across the room to rest upon a bronze relief on the wall behind the altar. Brom's eyes followed the beacon back to its source. The setting sunlight cast a radiant red glow around a ring of ancient symbols set into the central window. The cryptic circle was the same design that had been scrawled in the dust in the library.

Brom studied the macabre image set in the window glass. The blood-red circle surrounded a pale woman draped in black. A man lay bound on an altar before her, a dagger protruding from his chest. A stream of blood flowed from the wound, down over the altar and into a chalice below.

As Brom gazed upon the stained glass window, a bitter chill crept over him. Nightmarish images flooded his thoughts and a sinister scene began to form in his mind. He stood in the forest on a moonless night amidst the dark creatures of the brood. Ancient chants echoed through the trees, creating a primal, hypnotic rhythm as monstrous forms reveled in the surrounding shadows.

The demon queen, Lilith, stood atop an obsidian dais, presiding over the macabre ceremony. Draped in a shimmering ebony gown, her long, flowing hair matched the color of her raven-black eyes. In her right hand, she held a chalice, in her left she clutched a tarnished dagger. A young man lay motionless on an altar before her. Entranced and spellbound by the queen's dark sorcery, he stared helplessly into her eyes as she raised the dagger high above him. A hush befell the forest and the brood fell deathly silent for one brief moment. Lilith's black eyes opened wide as she plunged the blade deep into the man's chest. A stream of blood, dark and thick, pulsed from the fatal gash and the brood erupted in a savage uproar of howls and cackles. As her victim slowly expired, Lilith held a chalice beneath the wound to catch the crimson spill.

When at last death had claimed her victim, the Queen held the blood-filled chalice high for all to see, then drank deeply from it. After she had slaked her fiendish thirst, she passed the goblet to the frenzied horde. Reciting a mystical incantation, Lilith gestured a clawed hand downward and a blazing ring of crimson runes appeared on the ground before her. The earth beneath the arcane circle split open, revealing an entrance to the hidden underworld of the mountain. As the first rays of dawn threatened to illuminate the sky, the brood sought sanctuary in the deep shadows of the caverns below.

Returning to his own thoughts, Brom directed his gaze

once more to the halo of red light behind the chapel altar. The crimson runes came to rest upon a large circular design etched into a wall of tarnished bronze. Brom stepped forward, careful not to expose his flesh to the scalding sunlight. Investigating the bronze design, he noticed a small circular plate at the center of the engraving, fastened in place by hammered rivets. Brom took hold of the plate and pressed it, pushing on it from various directions in an attempt to turn it. At last the plate twisted to the side, revealing a hidden keyhole behind it.

Remembering the strange relic he had taken from the trespasser who had intruded upon his sanctuary long ago, Brom reached into the pocket of his cloak and withdrew the tarnished key he carried with him. He slipped the key into the hole and twisted it in the lock. With a screeching creak, the bronze panel split in two, opening into twin doors that slid away into the chapel wall. A cold breeze swept past him, filling Brom with unease and giving him the sensation that he had released some infernal spirit from its ancient prison. Peering into the cobwebbed shadows beyond the secret door, Brom discovered a hidden staircase leading down.

Heedless of what awaited in the darkness below, Brom entered the hidden passage. Thirteen stone steps circled down to a vaulted chamber lined with skulls and stacks of human bones. When he reached the bottom, he stood in the antechamber of the Tower's long-forgotten catacombs.

A tall figure stood silent and motionless at the far end of the chamber. Cloaked in the black robes of a monk, its face was concealed beneath the shadows of its hood. At first, Brom thought it was merely a statue adorning the crypt, but his senses alerted him to a spiritual presence. The figure stood before an arched passage leading into the catacombs, as if it were some ghostly sentinel at the threshold of the dead.

"Turn back," a low voice whispered, "lest ye fall victim to that which lurks below."

Still unsure whether the shadow monk was a spectral apparition or a physical being, Brom took a step closer. "Who are you?"

"I am the guardian of the gateway to the necropolis. Beyond this point lies the dark kingdom of the dead. It is hallowed ground, sanctified by the blood of martyrs. It is a sacred place, but also a haven for wayward souls. Hungry spirits wander these catacombs. They feed upon pain and sorrow, emptiness and grief. In the labyrinth far below, an ancient horror lies waiting."

As Brom took another step closer, the dark monk's voice raised to a raspy rumble that echoed round the crypt. "Heed my warning, Lord Brom. This path leads to suffering and ultimate darkness, though the answers you seek lie at its end. The choice remains yours, but consider your own fate before venturing forth into the depths of the abyss. The knowledge you seek has a costly price and there are consequences for every action."

Brom paused for a long moment to weigh the dark monk's words. At last, he reached his decision. "I can imagine nothing worse than spending eternity in this accursed place, for I have known only torment in my stay here. I must uncover all that lies hidden here, no matter the cost."

"So be it," the dark monk whispered. Without another word, the figure moved aside, allowing the Tower Lord free passage to the dark realms beyond.

Brom entered the corridor and followed the tunnel. The echo of his footfalls diminished with each step he took.

As the dark monk watched Brom disappear into the blackness of the crypt, a burning red glow spread through his eyes.

"Yes, Lord Brom," the shadow whispered, "Your destiny awaits... in the darkness far below."

Succubus

JOSEPH VARGO

Sheer black, stygian darkness surrounded Brom as he wandered deeper and deeper into the forgotten catacombs far below the Tower. The absence of light presented no obstacle to him, for he was now a creature of the night and he welcomed the embrace of shadows, but the network of winding corridors deprived him of his sense of direction, condemning him to wander aimlessly throughout the twisting maze. Each time he came upon an intersection, he raked his claw-like fingernails across the walls, scratching the sign of the cross into the cornerstones to mark his way. But the intertwining paths wrapped round themselves with no rhyme or reason, weaving back and forth at irregular intervals, and several times after walking for long periods Brom had come upon his own mark.

Though his body never grew weary, his spirit was temporarily weakened by the sense of sheer hopelessness presented by the endless series of corridors. For unknown durations he would walk, stopping only to reconsider his options, weighing the possibilities of continuing his mission, or forsaking it and turning around to find his way back to the surface. But his determination was fierce and each time doubt began to take root in his mind, he urged himself to tear free of its constricting hold and continued his quest with a freshly kindled resolve.

Brom was deep within the Tower's hidden underworld

now, and the tunnels curved and twisted at odd angles as the architecture became less and less familiar. The roughly chiseled granite walls gave way to smooth, polished marble and the passages became wider and taller, as if to accompany some ancient race of subterranean titans. The corridors themselves became more elaborate and ornamented, but the designs were unfamiliar to him. It was as though the deep tunnels had been crafted by master artisans of a long-forgotten era. As Brom ventured further into this newfound territory, a sensation of foreboding menace weighed heavily upon him, filling his heart with unease.

No sound permeated this realm of gloom and shadows far beneath the earth's surface. When he had first entered the catacombs, Brom could hear rats scurrying and water dripping in the distant tunnels, but now, once the echo of his footsteps dissipated, there were no other noises to be heard. The maddening silence of the grave reigned eternal within the ancient labyrinth.

Nearing the fringes of despair, Brom leaned back against the cold stone wall and slumped down to a seated position on the floor then closed his eyes to contemplate his situation. Allowing his mind to wander, he soon found himself lost in blissful reverie. A familiar memory took hold of his thoughts and his tension eased as he dreamt of his life long ago.

He lay upon a simple bed in a small house in Vasaria, warm and secure on a cold winter's night. A young village woman stood at the foot of his bed, silently watching over him in the dimly lit room. The meager light of the fireplace surrounded her dark hair with a soft amber glow, creating an ethereal aura that seemed to radiate from within her. Her eyes cast a hypnotic gaze, seductive in their innocence as they washed over his exposed chest and broad shoulders.

She stepped forward into the soft light, allowing him to admire her form as she leaned in close over him. Shadows caressed her tight-fitting bodice while the flickering light of the hearth's flame danced upon the curve of her bosom. Forgotten passions stirred deep within him as he reached out to touch her, longing to take her in his arms and feel her soft flesh next to his.

While the dream lasted, Brom relished the lost sensations of fragile mortality once again. And though the memory of his lost love was bittersweet, he cherished it and held it in his mind, keeping her forever with him.

Suddenly, a bitter chill swept over him, rousing Brom from his dream and alerting him to another presence nearby. He opened his eyes to catch a brief glimpse of a figure shrouded in white receding into the shadows at the far end of the corridor. Intrigued, but unsure of what he had witnessed, Brom slowly rose to his feet and stepped forth to investigate the dark passageway ahead, but as he turned the corner he found nothing there. He listened intently for the sound of footfalls retreating in the distance, but all was silent within the labyrinth. Staring into the empty void, Brom reasoned that the strange vision was nothing more than a remnant of his dream, but the inescapable feeling that he was no longer alone was too strong for him to deny.

Still curious, Brom proceeded to the next intersection, and once again he caught a fleeting glimpse of the mysterious phantom. Tendrils of flowing gossamer trailed behind the shrouded figure as it rounded the corner ahead. Brom rushed toward the intersection and turned the corner to confront the unknown entity, only to be met by empty shadows once more.

"Rianna!" Brom's voice echoed throughout the hollow

corridors as he called out to the memory of a woman killed long ago. Killed by his own blade, Brom reflected, ending her mortal life to spare her immortal soul. He stood mystified, staring into the darkness that surrounded him, pondering what he had seen, wondering if madness had begun to take hold of his mind.

Brom slowly proceeded further along the tunnel, the tragic memory of Rianna still haunting his thoughts. A series of sharp twists led to a narrow straightaway and there again Brom's eye caught the wisp of white silk as the specter vanished around the end of the corridor. He hastened his pace to pursue the elusive phantom, following the winding trail as the tunnels sloped downward, twisting deeper into the earth, but each time he rounded another corner, the ghostly form darted around the next, disappearing from sight. Again and again, he was met with no more than fleeting glimpses of the gossamer shroud as the mysterious figure led him further into the unknown depths of the ancient necropolis.

With each turn he felt certain he was closing in on the elusive specter, that the mysterious phantom would soon be within his grasp, but as he rounded the final corner, he was met with a stark revelation. He stood alone before a long corridor that culminated in a dead end. Ornate columns sculpted in the likeness of winged skeletons flanked the hallway and the corridor ended abruptly at an archway that had been sealed shut with stone and mortar. A single name was inscribed in the marble above the arch—a name that filled Brom with a sense of immortal dread. The inscription read "Lilith," marking the tomb as the final resting place of the Dark Queen's earthly remains.

Slowly and warily, Brom stepped toward the sealed archway at the end of the hall. As he walked between the skeletal angels that lined the corridor, he realized they were identical to the ones that guarded his sanctum door in the Tower above. The sculptures were eerily realistic, yet their intricate detail was lost to mortals' eyes, hidden deep inside the earth's slumbering darkness. As he proceeded beneath the hollow gazes of the grim stone sentinels, Brom felt irresistibly drawn to the sealed arch at the end of the hall, as if he were being summoned forth by some unearthly siren's call.

At last he came to stand before the ominous burial vault. Cautiously, Brom reached out to touch the bricks that sealed the crypt to verify that the tomb was indeed real and not merely a figment of a lucid dream. As soon as his fingertips rested upon the icy chamber walls, he was assaulted by an overwhelming sensation of sorrow and menace. Stumbling backward, Brom turned to flee, but a swirling cloud of black smoke and shadow filled the far end of the corridor, blocking his escape. The churning cloud crept toward him, engulfing him in its monstrous grasp and rendering him powerless. One by one, the skeletal statues that lined the hall turned their heads, casting their leering gazes toward him. Their deathly faces were the last thing Brom saw before his surroundings faded to black and he lapsed into oblivion.

When, at last, consciousness returned to him, Brom realized he was lying very still upon a cold stone slab in a vaulted chamber that had no apparent windows or doors. He tried to sit up but was unable to move. Though no physical bonds held him, he felt as if his arms and legs were shackled by heavy restraints. He was clothed in his crusader's garb from a life long past, his white longshirt hanging loose and unbuttoned, exposing his bare chest. As he became increasingly aware of his new surroundings, he felt a dark and ominous presence grow closer.

A billow of smoke began to rise from the mist that encircled the stone dais. Brom watched transfixed as the black cloud took the form of a beautiful dark angel draped in velveteen shadows. Raven-black hair cascaded down over her pale shoulders and ebony wings rose from her back, spreading outward behind her.

The unearthly creature seemed to float upon the air as she ascended the steps, approaching the altar where Brom lay helpless. Tendrils of her black gown delicately wavered behind her as she moved, trailing off into the tomb's shadows like vaporous serpents. The dark angel silently hovered beside him, and Brom shuddered as she placed a chilling hand upon his exposed chest. Beneath her icy touch, an unknown energy began to spread forth within his veins, and an unholy rapture claimed him as he lay paralyzed before her.

Unable to move and powerless to suppress the desires that stirred within him, Brom could not look away as the beautiful enchantress gazed down upon him. Staring into her hollow eyes, Brom realized he would not be set free by the angel of darkness that stood over him now. This unearthly creature was not his beloved Rianna—no. It was Mara, the Queen of Shadows.

Ever so slowly, Mara leaned over him, her luscious, red lips drawing closer to his. Unable to control the mortal passions she provoked within him, the temptation to taste her consumed Brom. For the briefest of moments, her lips brushed his, and as they did, Brom felt his will to resist crumble. No warmth emanated from within her, yet her slightest kiss had stirred Brom's darkest desires. He strained to reach towards her but his body was unable to break free of the sorcery that held him captive.

Mara raked her fingernails lightly across his chest in a

playful gesture that began as a gentle caress then swiftly ended in a moment of sharp pain. Although his body lay immobile and unresponsive, Brom could feel the searing cold of the wound that she had opened with her talons. Mara's black eyes glistened with savage delight as blood trickled from the slash. Brom's heart pounded furiously as he strained to fight the spell that bound him beneath her. While her unholy power filled his mind with terror, her irresistible beauty commanded his attention and kindled lustful desires deep within.

Mara slowly lowered her lips to the wound to taste its crimson spill but quickly drew back to cast a defiant glance to her side. Ghostly whispers echoed within the ancient tomb and the Dark Queen's black eyes searched for the unseen intruder.

When she seemed satisfied that she was alone with her prey, she leaned in close to Brom's ear and whispered softly, "At long last you have come to me."

The touch of her breath chilled him once again as Mara's voice echoed seductively. "I have lain dormant too long, imprisoned here in these abysmal depths. Once, I needed only to beckon, and men would grovel to heed my slightest whim. In pitiful Vasaria, they feared me. When young boys came of age, the village elders warned them of my lure. It was forbidden to venture beyond the standing stone that marked my domain. Yet each night, I visited them as they crossed the threshold of dreams. I allowed them to explore their darkest desires and left them hungering for more. I beckoned them to come to me—to fulfill their wicked fantasies. Those who could not resist my call were drawn to the Tower, to me... their ultimate fate. They were mere playthings for my amusement. But there was one who was different.

"He knew well the tales of the Dark Tower and what

had transpired there. His parents had warned him of Mara, the Queen of Shadows, and her unholy allegiance. They told him of the men and boys who went missing—how they had foolishly ventured into the Dark Queen's domain, drawn by her demon's call, never to return. But their tales only intrigued him and in time he came to me... for reasons of his own."

As the queen spoke, vivid visions began to fill Brom's head and he could see her tale play out in his mind's eye.

Dravek was his name. Born with eyes of palest grey and hair as white as December snow, he was marked as the Devil's own from the moment the village midwife first set eyes upon him. He was a sickly child, gaunt and prone to all manner of illness, and he was shunned by all who lived in Vasaria. He bore the vicious taunts of other children and the insults of the adults. Even his own parents eventually succumbed to the cruel tongues of the townsfolk and began to take their frustrations out on him. His young life was sheer torment. So unbearable was his existence that by the time he had reached his seventeenth year, he had made a decision to end his suffering, one way or another. Left with no one to console him and nothing to lose, he sought solace in the one place no one dared to visit. He ventured to the Tower.

He gathered his courage and made the trek up the winding mountain path, undeterred by the ravens that watched his every move beneath the scrutiny of their black, lifeless eyes. The frail boy gasped for breath as he reached the arched sentinel gate that spanned the overgrown road to the castle beyond. Still, he ventured forth.

At last he stood before the great doors of the Tower. He paused there for a long moment, wondering what unholy terrors might lay in wait within. Glancing back at the path behind him, he thought to flee for his pitiful life, but before he could act upon the impulse, the tower doors began to swing open, groaning on their ancient hinges. A whisper called to him from the darkness within, sending a chill down his spine, and Dravek stepped bravely forward to enter the forbidden keep.

No demons set upon him to drag him to Hell, nor was he assaulted by phantoms of the dead. Instead, a strange serenity encompassed him as he admired his gloom-shrouded surroundings. Elegant columns of black marble rose into the shadows overhead where nightmarish faces chiseled from stone peered down from the surrounding ledges and archways. The tower's sinister architecture left him awestruck, yet he felt strangely at home in the foreboding sanctuary of shadows.

Again, a soft whisper called to him, beckoning him deeper into the lurking darkness. Unable to resist the summoning call, Dravek crept across the chamber and slowly ascended a twisting staircase that swept upward to an overlooking balcony. He stood at the entrance to a grand hall illuminated by a few sparsely placed candles. At the far end of the chamber Mara reclined seductively upon her granite throne.

Dravek was well-versed in the tales of the Dark Queen and her ancient keep. This tower was hers. She had sacrificed her humanity to acquire it. She had murdered all who attempted to stand against her—even her own family. In this citadel of shadows, she reigned supreme, and the unfortunate few who dared to trespass upon her domain fell victim to her merciless wrath.

It was too late to turn back. Trembling, he approached the dais and dropped to one knee. Bowing his head before Mara, he quietly uttered his plea. "I seek an audience with you, my queen."

The cries of ravens erupted from the shadowed heights of the great hall. Their shrieking caws rose to a deafening crescendo then fell to an eerie hush as Mara began to speak.

"Throughout the long years, only a brave few have dared to cross the Tower's threshold, foolishly seeking their glory in my ruin." As she spoke, her voice echoed throughout the hall, surrounding Dravek with ghostly whispers. "I welcomed them all the same, for their blood served to slake my thirst and their flesh fed my hungry pets. Their bones lie scattered about you, where their restless spirits remain forever trapped. Their forlorn cries howl and wail in the night, as they lament their terrible fates."

Dravek raised his head to face the Dark Queen and stared deep into her cold, raven-black eyes. She returned his gaze with an icy stare that held him transfixed. Her unholy powers fascinated him and her dark beauty roused his innermost desires, yet being in her presence filled his heart with mortal terror. He knew his mission would end in death or damnation, but it mattered little to him.

Dravek closed his eyes and lowered his head once more. "I offer my life to you, and if you allow it, I shall live only to serve you."

"Your death would serve me just as well," Mara said as she raised a wicked smile, revealing the pointed tips of her fangs, "for there are few things I relish more than the taste of sweet young blood."

"Then end my life," Dravek uttered. "It matters not whether I live or die. This world shall not miss me."

Mara contemplated his words, then rose to her feet and stepped to the edge of the dais. She slowly descended the stone staircase, stopping directly in front of him.

"Look upon me," she commanded.

Dravek's eyes slowly washed over every nuance of her voluptuous body.

"Once I was of the same mind," Mara's voice purred seductively. "Long ago, I too felt lost in the shadows of this cruel world, but I was guided by a dark savior." Mara leaned in close to Dravek's face and brushed his white hair aside then whispered softly in his ear. "I can be your savior, but like me, you must first prove your dedication."

Dravek had learned early on to bear great torments, burying his pain deep inside, where it simmered and festered into a twisted hatred of his fellow man. But unlike the cruel jests and unending ridicule that had spawned his disdain for humanity, Mara's words filled his heart with the feeling of acceptance that he had never before known.

"You need only name a task, and it shall be done."

A smile formed on Mara's lips as she ascended the steps to return to her throne. She leaned back against the cold granite and locked her black eyes on Dravek. "What do you cherish most in this world?"

"There is nothing I cherish but you, my queen. No one else matters to me."

"What of your parents, your family, your friends?"

"They mean nothing to me. I have no friends."

"Surely there must be someone that bears you some extent of mortal compassion."

Dravek hesitated, then said at last, "Yes, there is one—a village girl—Liliana is her name. She is different from the others. At times she has shown pity on me."

"Pity?" Mara's eyes narrowed as she spat the word. "Kings are not pitied, nor do they show mercy. Your potential is limitless, but you must first realize your true nature."

Mara raised her arm and a raven swooped from the shadows to perch upon her wrist. She gently stroked her nails across the bird's ebon plumes and the raven's eyes filled with a crimson glow. "I shall entrust you with a simple task. I shall allow you to leave here with your wretched life. If you are content to suffer the torments of your pitiful existence and remain the lowly subject of the villager's ignorant contempt, so be it." Mara made a slight gesture with her outstretched hand and the raven left her wrist to perch upon the top of her throne. "But should you truly desire to rise above the mortal squalor to take your place at my side, return to the Tower on the eve of the full moon with this girl who finds you pitiful."

"And what shall become of her?" Dravek regretted the foolishness of his question before it had left his lips.

Mara sprang to her feet, gnashing her fangs like a savage beast. "Do not question your master!" Her voice sent an unearthly echo throughout the hall. The Dark Queen stood at the edge of the dais, glaring down at the terror-stricken boy until at last she regained her composure. "I assure you, I shall do nothing to harm her," she said calmly. "Now go."

Without another word, Dravek fled the Tower and rushed back to the village.

On the eve of the next full moon, he ventured up the forest path once again, this time bringing Liliana with him. Filling her head with tales of treasure, Dravek kindled the girl's curiosity to investigate the forbidden keep. They passed no ravens along their way through the grim woodlands and as they approached the castle, the great doors stood open, as if the Tower were awaiting their arrival.

With Dravek leading the way, the two silently entered the ancient fortress. Beams of moonlight shone down through the windows of the entrance hall, offering pale patches of illumination between regions of abysmal darkness. When they reached the center of the chamber, they were greeted by a voice from the shadows.

"Welcome, children." The queen's words echoed throughout the empty chamber and one by one, the torches on the surrounding columns burst into flames, bathing the hall in an auburn glow. As the darkness receded, Mara appeared on the balcony overlooking the room. A black velvet gown adorned with blood-red scrollwork clung to her body like a second skin.

"We have been awaiting you." The queen raised her arms, directing her guests' attention above her. Dravek and the girl gazed in awe at the canopy of writhing shadows that loomed overhead. Scores of ravens filled the heights of the great hall, nestled among the gargoyles and grotesques. Deathly silent and black as sin, the frightful birds glared down at them with gleaming ruby eyes.

Stricken with terror, Liliana turned to flee but froze in place when she saw that her escape was blocked. An unearthly mist filled the doorway and more crimson eyes glistened from the darkness beyond. As the eerie fog crept toward them and spread throughout the entrance hall, the shadowy forms of wolves emerged from the haze. Dravek and the girl stood petrified as the hellish creatures surrounded them, growling and poised to attack.

The wind whistled through the open doorway, giving rise to a mournful wail that echoed throughout the chamber. When the howling cry subsided, Mara recited an ominous verse.

"Wolves and ravens share the night,
an omen for the morrow—
The wind carries the banshee's cry
to foretell coming sorrow—"

The Dark Queen laughed with wicked delight. "My dear boy, how it pleases me to see that you have returned." Mara's black eyes shifted to Liliana. "And you did not come alone." The queen's eyes narrowed as she stared into the depths of the girl's soul, then her ebon gaze returned to Dravek. "You have done well," she proudly declared, "very well indeed. Now I shall give you a final choice. You can remain with this simple girl and meet your fate as you had previously wished, or you can take your place at my side and explore a realm of untold desires."

Dravek stared blankly at the girl. Her eyes welled with tears as she begged him to help her, but he ignored her sobbing pleas and turned away. The wolf pack parted before him, allowing him to leave the surrounding circle. Slowly and warily, he proceeded between their snarling ranks. The savage beasts let him pass, then closed the gap behind him, reforming their encompassing ring around Liliana.

Ascending the Tower staircase, Dravek stepped to the Dark Queen's side. "Do what you will with her, my queen." His voice rang cold and hollow.

Mara smiled. "As I have said, I shall do nothing to harm her. My wolves are now yours to command. A sacrifice must be made to attain what you desire most."

Dravek stared down at the helpless girl who had befriended and trusted him.

Mara stroked Dravek's head, running her nails through his long hair. "Her heart holds no feelings for you. She merely pities you. True power knows no mercy."

Dravek surrendered to the Dark Queen's will and relinquished his last shreds of humanity. With a nod he signaled the wolves to attack, and the vicious beasts obeyed his silent command.

Liliana screamed with terror as the pack converged on her but her cries were soon silenced by the wolves at her throat. Mara's dark eyes glistened as she watched the frenzied creatures feast upon the girl's young flesh. "We shall share a great future together," she whispered. "Those who have shunned us shall know our vengeance. Fate has brought you to me for a reason."

Dravek watched over the grisly scene below with sinister glee. The notion of casting those who had tormented him to the hungry wolves brought a twisted smile to his face. Yes, he thought, Vasaria would pay dearly for all it had done to him. In time, they would all know his wrath. In time, they would all suffer.

Brom's vision faded to darkness and he found himself standing before Mara's tomb once more. A quick scan of his surroundings revealed nothing but shadows lurking in the bleak depths of the catacombs. The skeletal statues that flanked the hall watched over the empty corridor in deathly silence.

Images swarmed his mind and memories whirled around him as he tried to make sense of all that had transpired. Looking down at his clothes, he saw that he was dressed in the same black tunic and cloak he had been wearing when he entered the tunnels below the Tower. He reached beneath his shirt and felt his chest for the wound Mara had opened, but there was no injury or scar. Everything that happened from the moment he first laid hands upon the Dark Queen's crypt had been nothing more than a terrible dream—a nightmarish vision conjured by Mara's unholy sorcery.

Brom now knew the truth. He had discovered the sinister secret of the catacombs—the undying evil that lay entombed here at the labyrinth's end—and he vowed to sacrifice his life and soul, if need be, in order to keep the Dark Queen from ever rising again. He turned from Mara's tomb, but before he could take a step, a whisper crept from the darkness behind him. The faint sound rose to a ghostly murmur that seemed to call his name. He felt the icy caress of cold fingers sprawling across his chest, and he shuddered as Mara's final words echoed inside his head. "Fate has brought you to me for a reason."

The Ghost at The Sepulchre

JOSEPH VARGO

Far beneath the Dark Tower, in a forsaken realm of shadows, Brom walked alone. Engulfed in the infernal gloom and maddening silence of the crypt, he trod wearily through the twisting tunnels that led back to the surface. He had discovered the ancient lair hidden deep inside the mountain, and he had survived his encounter with the undying horror that lay entombed at the black heart of the maze. Now, as he began his long trek back, Brom cursed his own recklessness and brazen curiosity for prodding him to venture so far from the sanctum of the keep. Leaving the abysmal depths of the labyrinth behind, he followed his trail back through the catacombs toward the Tower above.

Time lapsed and drifted in the ancient tunnels. Weeks, perhaps months had transpired since he began his quest to explore the Tower's hidden underworld. Perhaps it had been even longer. Here in the forgotten necropolis where unrelenting darkness prevailed over the countless centuries, all sense of time was lost.

Trudging further, Brom began to recognize familiar markers along the stone corridors. When he first descended into the maze of winding passages, he had marked his path by scratching crosses into the tunnel walls. As he retraced his steps through the catacombs, his eyes sought the guiding symbols etched into the dark stone. The crosses appeared with greater frequency as he gradually drew closer to the surface.

Though Brom's unearthly vision allowed him to see clearly in the pitch-blackness, his sight was limited to shades of blue. Turning a corner, he spied a faint glimmer in the tunnel ahead. Brom slowed his pace, stepping cautiously along a corridor lined with human skulls. Long devoid of the souls that once inhabited them, their hollow eyes stared lifelessly into the dark as Brom passed by. He followed the twisting passage to a gated archway framing a crypt carved into the bedrock. Brom had noticed the lavish burial vault when he first entered the catacombs. Upon his descent, the vault stood dark and deathly still, but now a strange light radiated from within, filling the crypt with a shimmering glow.

Stepping slowly to the iron gate that sealed the crypt's entrance, Brom peered into the vault. He stood in silent awe, mesmerized by the sight before him. A beautiful young woman with golden hair leaned over an ornate sepulchre chiseled from black stone. She gazed longingly at the sculpture of a winged skeleton that adorned the tomb's lid. The girl's hair and silken gown gently wavered in the air behind her like vaporous tendrils of pale smoke and her radiant form cast a soft glow around her. This was no living person, Brom surmised, but the spectral form of a long-dead soul, lost in the crypt's consuming darkness.

The lovely phantom hovered above the sculpted angel, tenderly caressing its skeletal fingers with her own. Brom stood entranced by the strange ritual he was witnessing, yet he could not fathom its meaning. Perhaps, he thought, this wandering ghost merely longed for the Angel of Death to release her from the confines of the grave, to guide her wayward spirit to its eternal rest in the kingdom of the afterlife. But this was not to be.

Brom took hold of the gate latch and tried to turn it quietly, but the corroded handle was frozen in place. The rusted gate relinquished a slight creak, drawing the spectre's attention. The apparition turned her head toward the crypt's sealed threshold, setting her lifeless gaze upon Brom. The phantom rose and backed away from the tomb, vanishing into the solid stone wall at the far side of the crypt. Brom wrenched the gate handle downward, twisting the latch until the rusted lock gave way. With a groaning squeal, the decrepit gate swung open and Brom stepped warily forward to investigate the forgotten burial vault.

The chamber held an icy chill, more frigid and harsh than the dead of winter. Brom's eyes swept across the black sepulchre, examining the details of the macabre monument. The skeletal angel that lay in deathly repose upon the tomb's lid was identical to the grim statues that stood silent vigil throughout the Tower and catacombs. A stone nameplate adorned the foot of the sepulchre, but the plaque held no inscription. With each new detail Brom discovered, he grew more and more intrigued by the mysterious crypt.

Though no name marked the tomb, a Latin inscription ran along the side of the stone sarcophagus. Brom brushed his fingers across the dusty engraving chiseled into the black marble: *LIBERA ANIMUS OMNIUM FIDELIUM DEFUNCTORUM DE POENIS OBSCURUM.*

Translating the phrase to the best of his knowledge, Brom whispered the words, "Free the souls of the faithful departed from pain and darkness."

As he circled the stone coffin, he discovered the decaying remnants of a human skeleton heaped in the corner of the room. Long golden strands flowed from the skull and a tattered silken gown covered the rotting bones. There was little doubt in Brom's mind that the remains were those of the beautiful apparition who stood watch over the tomb.

Brom's curiosity plagued him. Unable to ignore the macabre mystery, he sought to resolve it. Placing his hands upon the sepulchre lid, he pushed it aside. The heavy slab grated across the stone coffin as it slid open, emitting a gust of ancient, stale air and revealing the tomb's morbid contents. Another skeleton lay inside the sepulchre. The entombed bones were much larger than those of the skeleton on the floor. The remains of a man, Brom deduced. The corpse clutched a scroll between its withered fingers. Brom blessed himself, making the sign of the cross, and pried the tattered parchment from the dead man's bony grasp. Unrolling the primitive document, Brom discovered a strange epitaph, penned in an ancient hand.

Here lies the body of Victor, faithful son of Vasaria and devoted servant of Queen Mara. His tale is chronicled here for all to know the tragic circumstances of his untimely fate. Let it be known to those who read this that Victor met his death in the Tower, sacrificing his life for the love of his queen. Having fallen beneath Mara's spell of immortal beauty, he surrendered his heart to her. Enchanted by the Queen's unearthly charms, Victor professed his undying love to her, and in doing so, he sealed his own fate.

A village girl named Gabriella, who coveted Victor for herself, ventured to the Tower in pursuit of her heart's desire. She longed for Victor, wanting nothing other than to be his wife. But Victor did not return the girl's affections, scoffing at her foolish wishes and childish notions of love. For that, he felt her murderous rage. Her jealous hand brought him to his end, delivering a dagger to pierce his heart, destroying the very thing she could not possess. With his dying breath, he cursed the lowly girl to wander the bleak shadows of the earth until the end of time.

In her grief, Queen Mara sentenced the girl to death for her

*murderous deed and Gabriella was condemned to be entombed
alive in the catacombs beneath the Tower. May her soul suffer in
eternal darkness.*

As Brom read the final words, the ghostly glow returned to
illuminate the crypt. Turning slowly, he saw that the spectre
had reappeared behind him. The beautiful phantom stood in
the tomb's doorway, stretching her arms across the opening,
blocking Brom's exit.

"Be gone, spirit," Brom said, his deep voice resounding in
the hollow chamber like thunder. "Leave this tomb and meet
your damnation."

The spectre floated nearer, hovering in the air before Brom.
Her ashen face held a look of devastating sadness.

A feeling of sympathy welled in Brom's heart and his harsh
tone softened. "Your eternal fate has been cast. I can offer you no
solace, nor redemption for your sins."

The spectre's pale eyes glistened as if she were weeping, but
she conveyed no words. She drifted to the side of the sepulchre,
wrapping her arms around the lid as she looked down at the
withered body within. She lifted her head toward Brom, her
eyes pleading some unspoken message, like a helpless animal
caught in an inescapable trap.

Brom stepped to the sepulchre and stared across the
sculpted angel of death, locking his eyes upon the tormented
spirit. His gaze penetrated her consciousness and Brom
peered deep into her soul. As he did, a vision began to form
in his mind.

Brom saw the spirit as she was long ago, before her mortal
life came to an end. Carefree and innocent, she walked alone
through the forest outside Vasaria, picking wildflowers to wear

in her hair. Though still a child at heart, she had blossomed into a radiant beauty and now stood at the threshold of womanhood. Reaching a grassy clearing, she met a young man, handsome and lean. She ran to his waiting arms and pressed her lips against his. They tumbled to the grass beneath the shade of a willow tree, where they lay nestled in each other's loving embrace. The young couple shared their dreams of a future together, unaware of the figure that stood nearby, silently watching them from the shadows of the forest.

Twilight was soon upon them. As the sun sank beneath the horizon, ghostly grey forms crept forth from the dark woodlands, stealthily surrounding the unwary couple. The sound of low growling roused the couple from their blissful reverie, alerting them to the encompassing danger. Six wolves encircled them in the tall grass, blocking all possible paths of escape. The fearsome creatures stood motionless—snarling, but frozen in place, as if awaiting some unseen master's command.

A man cloaked in black stood at the edge of the forest. Though his face was hidden beneath the shadows of his hood, his eyes reflected the crimson blaze of the setting sun.

"Come with me," the dark figure hissed. Without another word, the shadow turned and retreated along the forest path that led toward the Dark Tower.

The wolves drew closer, baring their savage fangs, prompting the young man and woman to follow their mysterious guide. The captive couple trod woefully along the mountain path toward the ominous black citadel that loomed high upon the summit. Upon reaching their destination, the cloaked man lit a torch and escorted his prisoners inside the unhallowed fortress, leading them to the royal hall. The wolf pack stopped at the chamber's threshold and stood guard outside the doorway, their eyes aglow like burning embers.

Darkness greeted the couple and their guide inside the chamber—an absolute sprawling blackness that their eyes could not penetrate. The cloaked man bowed his head and stood silent.

The Queen's voice echoed through the cavernous hall. "A thousand eyes have I, peering from the abyss. Unseen, yet ever vigilant, my servants stand watch from the shadows. Within my domain, nothing escapes my notice."

Torches suddenly blazed along marble columns lining the walls, casting an amber glow throughout the desolate chamber, illuminating the room's hidden horrors. Human bones lay scattered about the floor amidst scores of restless ravens. Disturbed by the torchlight, the black birds took flight, seeking sanctuary in the chamber's shadowed heights.

At the far end of the room, atop a tiered dais, Mara sat in her ancient throne. A corseted gown clung to her pale flesh, draping her voluptuous form in black velvet. Spikes of wrought iron rose like tall thorns from the crown that rested upon her head. One hand stroked the sleek feathers of a raven that stood perched upon the arm of her throne, while her other hand clutched a tarnished goblet.

Mara's black eyes narrowed. "What have we here?"

"Trespassers, my queen," the cloaked figure answered.

Mara rose from her throne. "Who dares to violate my decree?"

"I am Victor, a simple blacksmith in Vasaria," the young man said quietly, then gestured to the girl beside him, "and this is Gabriella. We were in the forest together. We did nothing wrong."

A raspy whisper emanated from the shadowed cowl of the cloaked man. "They crossed the boundary of the standing stone, my queen."

Mara's pitiless gaze found Victor. "It is forbidden to venture beyond the ancient threshold without my consent," she stated coldly.

Victor's face betrayed a look of dire concern. "We did not know we were on hallowed ground," he said. "Forgive us. We meant no harm or disrespect."

Mara's soulless eyes washed over Victor's body, caressing his muscular form. "Step forth," she commanded.

The young man slowly advanced to the base of the steps leading to the Queen's throne. Mara descended the staircase, stopping one step above Victor. She raised her pale hand to his face, gently sweeping his jet-black hair behind his ear. Her clawed fingers stroked his shoulders, running along his collarbone and slipping down across his chest. Using one sharp nail, she sliced through the front of his shirt, then ran her fingers lightly up his exposed stomach, softly brushing against his lean muscles.

Mara slid her tongue across her crimson lips in a manner unbefitting royalty. Victor stood speechless and rapt beneath her hypnotic gaze. She glanced away and Victor gasped for breath.

The Queen spoke quietly. "A fire stirs within you. You have felt its heat, but you have yet to know the extent of its flames. Your simple mind cannot fathom the true depths of ecstasy. Allow me to guide you along the path of desire. Relinquish yourself to me and you will know pleasures beyond earthly compare."

Victor kept his head lowered, averting his eyes from Mara's spellbinding stare. "My heart is spoken for, my queen. I have asked Gabriella to be my bride. We are betrothed to be married when the harvest moon rises."

Rage welled within Mara's eyes. "You dare put your affections for this simple wench before the love of your queen?

She is a mere child, ignorant and meek, unworthy of trodding the same ground I walk." Mara cast her fierce gaze upon the terrified girl. "Do you see how she trembles in my presence? Her very life rests upon my whims. If I were to but wish her gone, she would be no more."

"Please," Victor said, his voice shaking, "she has done nothing wrong. Spare her, I beg of you. Punish me as you will, but do not harm her. I will do anything you wish, but I cannot betray my heart."

"Ah, the reckless folly of love." Mara's words burned with a subtle mocking tone. "It gives rise to courage beyond all reason, stirring a boldness of the spirit when all hope seems lost." The ire in her eyes subsided. "Your words have moved me, young Victor." She set her hand upon her pale chest. "They have touched the very core of my being and inspired me. If you have bequeathed your heart to this simple girl, then so be it.

"I ask but one thing of you—a simple task," Mara said softly, "a humble token of devotion to your queen. Do this, and I shall set you free. Your wishes shall be honored. You and your love shall be together—forever united by my decree."

A look of relief swept across Victor's face. "Name the task and it shall be done," he said, "no matter the obstacle or hazard."

A sly grin formed upon the Dark Queen's lips. "As I have said, it is but a simple task." Mara held forth the tarnished chalice. "I would have you fill this goblet to slake my vexing thirst."

Victor took the blackened chalice from her hand, saying, "I shall fill it with the finest wine, in your honor, my queen."

"Wine?" Mara laughed, sending sinister cackles echoing around the vaulted chamber.

Setting her clawed hands on Victor's shoulders she turned him to face Gabriella. Pulling him back toward her, Mara held her captive close to her breast. He could not fight her unearthly strength, had he dared to resist her. Her left hand pressed against his chest, holding him tightly in place while the clawed fingers of her right hand slowly sprawled across his throat like the legs of a deadly spider.

"I thirst not for wine." Mara's words rang cold and hollow. She swept a single claw across Victor's throat, opening a thin line in his flesh. A stream of scarlet began to drip from the cut.

"No!" Gabriella screamed, dropping to her knees in a cascade of uncontrollable sobs.

Mara's cloaked minion clutched the girl by her hair and yanked her head upward, forcing her to watch the grisly spectacle before her. Victor's eyes stared wide in horror as his life's essence seeped from his throat. Mara pressed her palm against his forehead, slowly tilting his head back, allowing his blood to flow freely.

As Victor's strength slipped away, Mara took the chalice from his hand. She held the goblet beneath the wound, catching the crimson flow that pulsed from the dying man's neck. Victor's legs buckled beneath him and his weight slumped against Mara. The Dark Queen released him from her grasp and his body sunk heavily to the floor. Raising the blood-filled chalice to her mouth, Mara drank deeply, savoring its sanguine contents.

The Dark Queen knelt behind her helpless victim. She stroked her clawed fingers through Victor's hair and lowered her bloodstained lips to his ear. "Worry not," she whispered, "your precious love will not be harmed—this I assure you. She will be with you always."

Mara laid her hand upon Victor's chest, digging her black nails into his flesh. In one swift action, she plunged her talons beneath his ribcage, ripping his yet-beating heart from his body. Streams of deep crimson trickled between her bone-white fingers. Mara held the bloody trophy before her eyes and watched as it pulsed to a halt.

The Dark Queen rose and stood over her vanquished prey, the fury of Hell simmering behind her black eyes. Slowly, she turned to face Gabriella. The Queen stepped forward, holding her blood-drenched arm outstretched, offering the grisly contents of her hand as a gift.

"He bequeathed this to you," Mara said, discarding Victor's heart at the girl's feet. "It was his wish that you and you alone have it."

Gabriella recoiled in revulsion, but there was no escape from the nightmare that encompassed her. Nearing madness, her rasping screams filled the hall, stirring the ravens from their roosts high above.

During the dead of night, the Dark Queen set forth upon the final acts of her villainous scheme. Victor's body was taken to the catacombs and entombed within the sepulchre that was constructed for Mara's father, the ancient king of the realm. Mara related a false account of Victor's death to her scribe, corrupting the truth to create her own story, claiming Gabriella murdered Victor in a jealous rage. Mara's twisted account was transcribed on the scroll, and the parchment was sealed inside Victor's tomb.

Mara then sentenced Gabriella to a ghastly fate, condemning her spirit to forever wander the forsaken shadows of the earth. The girl was dragged to the catacombs and buried alive, locked in the crypt that held Victor's body. Gabriella spent her last days struggling in vain to pry open the immense lid in an attempt to retrieve the deceitful scroll, but she possessed not the strength to move the heavy stone. Starved and weakened beyond hope, she drew her last breath at the foot of the sepulchre, but her soul could find no release from its torment. Her spirit remained trapped in the earthly realm, bound to the crypt until the truth of Victor's death was revealed.

The vision dissolved and Brom returned to his own thoughts. The spectre cast her woeful gaze upon Victor's withered body one final time, then slowly faded from sight. Brom shuddered at the thought of Mara's monstrous deception. Because she could not sway Victor's heart from a mere mortal woman, the demon queen unleashed her merciless wrath upon them. It was not enough for her to sentence the innocent lovers to a horrific death, she reveled in their eternal torment, condemning them to remain forever separated in the afterlife as well. Her cruelty knew no limits.

Brom could still feel Gabriella's presence in the tomb. Her plight was not yet resolved. Knowing that her spirit would not rest until her body was given a proper burial, Brom set the girl's remains inside the sepulchre to lie beside her beloved Victor. He sealed the sarcophagus and dug his sharp nails into the plaque at the base of the tomb, etching their names into the stone.

When he had finished, he stood over the tomb and bowed his head in silent prayer. "Victor and Gabriella—together till the end of time." His whispered words echoed in the lonely vault. "May you finally know peace."

Closing the crypt gate behind him, Brom resumed his trek back to the Tower. The tunnels soon became less tangled and easier to navigate. With each step, Brom felt as if someone were following him. At times he would feel a bitter chill at his back, but looking behind him, he saw nothing. Venturing onward, he found his way back to the vaulted chamber at the base of the Tower stairs. The ghostly monk that stood vigil when Brom entered the catacombs was nowhere to be seen and the chamber appeared empty, but once again, an eerie coldness crept over him.

At long last Brom returned to the surface, emerging in the Tower's chapel. The first rays of dawn broke through the stained glass windows, casting radiant colors upon the tiled floor. During his time in the catacombs, Brom had dreamt of seeing daylight once again, but now as he stood surrounded by its blinding spectrum, he was reminded of its deadly, searing caress. Sealing the catacomb entrance behind him, Brom made his way through the chapel, keeping to the shadows along the chamber's western wall.

He retreated to the confines of his library sanctum and set quill to parchment to document his discoveries in the Tower's forgotten underworld, taking special care to chronicle the true tale of the lovers who met their terrible fates at the savage hands of the Dark Queen. Once more, Brom felt the chilling presence that had followed him from the catacombs. His eyes darted around the shadows of the chamber, but he found no one there.

Brom stepped before the hearth and lit a small fire. As the flames lapped at the kindling, a soft blue glow emanated from the opposite side of the room. Brom turned to see the beautiful spectre standing behind him, the silken tendrils of her gown wavering in the frosty air. Reaching beneath his cloak, Brom withdrew the scroll he had taken from the tomb. He let the parchment fall from his hand and the spirit's solemn eyes followed the page as it drifted into the fire. As the scroll dwindled to ashes in the consuming flames, the look of sadness left the phantom's face. The room grew warmer, losing its frigid chill, and Gabriella's spirit vanished into the darkness one final time.

The Seventh Chalice

Joseph Iorillo and Joseph Vargo

At first, Adrian thought they had lost the path. The forest's undergrowth had become more treacherous and the dying sun had left them in almost total darkness. As the land rose sharply, the cobblestones of the path became increasingly obscured by moss and withered roots. Adrian's horse reluctantly pressed forward. Ahead, Leonidas spurred his steed over a thicket of thorny vines and glanced behind him at his old friend.

"Not far," Leonidas said, his breath pluming out in a grey, chilly cloud. The temperature had dropped considerably as they neared the Tower.

Adrian nodded, not quite trusting the old man's navigational instincts. However, soon they reached a clearing dominated by a dilapidated stone gateway. Upon the three arches a flock of ravens perched, silently staring at the two intruders. Beyond the arches, the mountain rose sharply, blending almost seamlessly into the black stone angles and curves of the Dark Tower.

The last embers of the setting sun succumbed to the purple and indigo clouds on the horizon, and the arrival of night seemed to agitate the carrion birds. The ravens suddenly took flight in a raucous fury of beating wings. They soared upward toward the Tower, in an uproar of ghastly croaking.

It was not only the chilly autumnal air that was making Adrian uncomfortable. Leonidas seemed to divine his unease even in the darkness. "Do you think I lead you to harm?" the old man said, smiling slightly. "Remember—this was your wish."

Adrian answered by nudging his anxious horse on further. Soon they arrived at the Tower, and Adrian was surprised to see the massive oak doors of the keep standing open, as if the two old men had been expected.

Once again, Leonidas appeared to read his friend's mind. "The ravens have announced our arrival," Leonidas said. "The lord of the Tower has assessed whether or not we are a threat. Let us proceed."

It took a moment before Adrian was able to summon the courage to mount the steps and follow his friend into the blackness of the Tower.

They found themselves in the cavernous entryway, the air thick with ancient dust. The only illumination came from the crescent moon, visible in one of the narrow casements. Adrian's eye was drawn to the balcony overlooking the entrance hall. A thin figure of a man stood there, watching them.

Once again, Adrian felt his courage flagging. He had fought a generation ago in the Holy Land; he had killed marauding Moslems who had raided his camp in the dead of night. Still, the crypt-like atmosphere of this infernal place unnerved him beyond all measure.

Leonidas called out to the figure above them. "My lord, I bring to you Brother Adrian, from the Priory of St. Sebastian." The old man's voice echoed in the immense circular chamber. "He is an old friend who had grown up in Vasaria. He requires assistance that only you may be able to provide."

The silhouette upon the balcony said nothing, but Adrian could feel the creature's eyes upon him.

"Our monastery lies half a day's journey to the south," Adrian said, his voice hoarse and faltering. "We are but humble servants of the Lord, but our history has more than its share of tragedy. Many years ago, a small group of our order unearthed an ancient scroll hidden deep within a forgotten chamber in our burial vaults. They kept this discovery a secret as they struggled to interpret the message contained on the parchment. The sacrilegious writings of the scroll...." Adrian's voice had withered to a husky whisper, and he cleared his throat. "What these brothers found somehow changed them, corrupting their faith.

"They soon began unnatural practices and held arcane rituals during the dead of night. During their unholy communion, human blood was spilled—an offering to dark powers as they strove to summon the Fallen Ones. Before they could do so, the blood cult's macabre plans were discovered and their hideous ritual was thwarted. The brothers were tried, and though they professed their innocence, they were burned at the stake for their heresy. I was not present for this." Adrian felt it necessary to impart this last fact. He had been the lone dissenting voice in the order during the trial, trying in vain to remind the others of their Christian duty to preserve life, even the lives of those consumed by wickedness. "The scroll was ultimately locked away in our library, sealed within the artifact vault, and it was forbidden to look upon it."

"Three nights ago, however, the seal was broken and the scroll is now missing. A phantom now haunts the monastery's halls—a dark spirit that is believed to be an entity summoned forth from Hell, by someone using the scroll's illicit magic. A young village girl was found murdered, her body laid across the cathedral altar. Her blood was drained to fill seven chalices that surrounded her. Upon her white flesh, drawn in her own blood, was a symbol that none could decipher. I alone recognized the twisted rune, recalling it from my youth. For it was the symbol of the Tower, the emblem of the dark lord of Vasaria."

For the first time, Lord Brom spoke, his voice the fearsome

murmur of someone accustomed to living among brooding shadows and silence. "What are you saying?"

"I accuse you of nothing, Lord Brom," Adrian replied, unnerved to hear the legendary creature speak. "Leonidas has told me of you, and I know of your vigil here. I bring you my tale to seek your help, for surely this emblem was left for you. We beseech you to come to the cathedral and vanquish this evil as you have done with that which once held dominion in this place."

"My mission lies within this tower," Brom said. "I cannot leave here."

Leonidas looked apologetically at Adrian. "We can offer aid, but we dare not allow Lord Brom to be lured away and leave the Tower unguarded."

Adrian peered more intently at Brom. "Leonidas has told me of your quest to resolve the mysteries of this place. Perhaps our monastery's plight will lead to some of the answers you seek. Our library is vast and our catacombs are older than those beneath the Tower. Many secrets lie buried there."

Brom said nothing. In the dimness, Adrian saw Brom's eyes move from the two guests to the massive inlaid symbol in the flagstones upon which Leonidas and Adrian stood. "The vigil must be maintained," Brom murmured, "I must remain here."

Leonidas took Adrian's elbow and led his old friend to the door. Reluctantly, the monk allowed himself to be led away. Angry and disappointed, Adrian felt on the verge of tears. The trip had been for naught, and now the Priory would succumb to the diabolic embrace of the evil unleashed there. It was as if a blasphemous shadow had fallen upon his world and everything he held dear.

As they were about to step out into the night, Adrian heard Brom's low voice again. "Wait." The word echoed through the chamber.

Adrian and Leonidas exchanged a look, then waited as

Brom's sharp footfalls rang out above them and marked his descent to the entrance hall. Adrian's unease deepened as Lord Brom strode to him, his fierce, glistening eyes never wavering as they appraised the monk with the coldness of a predator smelling blood. Suddenly, his eyes flicked over to Leonidas. The old man seemed to recoil. "You both shall return here at dusk tomorrow, with a boy from the village—the one named Lorand. He shall become my emissary and act on my behalf. I shall bestow upon him the knowledge and means to combat the spirit tormenting the Priory. Tell no one of this plan. And both you and the boy should clothe yourselves in the garb of the monks."

"Why?" Adrian boldly asked.

Brom once again focused on the monk. "If you truly desire my help, you will do as I say." The Lord of the Tower withdrew once more into the shadows, and Adrian was startled to hear the unearthly cries of the ravens behind him. The black birds had alighted on the top of the massive door, their jewel-like eyes peering menacingly at the two interlopers. Their wings beat madly, as if signaling to the old men that their audience with Lord Brom was at an end. Leonidas firmly took his friend's arm and led him out into the windy night to their horses.

On the ensuing evening, the trek to the Dark Tower was even more perilous, as a heavy mist lay over the forest and mountain, obscuring the path and disorienting their trio of stallions. Leonidas led the way, his torch flickering meagerly in the fog, and behind him rode Adrian, hunched low in his thick cowl. Shivering in the frigid air, he glanced behind him at Lorand, the young stablehand from Vasaria whom Leonidas knew and trusted. The solemn young man had not shown any trepidation when Leonidas had asked him to accompany them to the accursed Tower; in fact, the boy's serious face had hardened with grim resolve and he nodded with enthusiasm, agreeing to clothe himself in an old cloak that resembled Adrian's cowl. Adrian attributed the boy's eagerness to the rashness of youth, for Adrian himself had been headstrong when young. Headstrong and hungry for adventure—even if the adventure could be deadly.

Lorand was nothing more than a dark, hooded silhouette upon horseback. Adrian could not see his face, nor could he see much of the path before him. As they neared the Tower, visibility seemed to degrade even further and gnarled branches and bushes loomed out of the darkness, resembling silent monsters. The old monk chastised himself for being so frequently startled by them.

When the three cloaked figures finally escaped the cold, windy evening and stood in the entrance hall of the Dark Tower, Adrian was shocked to see Lord Brom already awaiting them. Standing like a fierce, caped statue upon the sigil embedded upon the stone floor, Brom held up a pale hand, halting the three in their tracks by the door. Brom's eyes peered into the hoods of their cloaks, seeing first Adrian, then the elder Leonidas, then the boy.

Despite being on the verge of manhood, Lorand seemed to cower in his robes, shivering more than either Adrian or Leonidas. Adrian's heart went out to the boy, upon whom Brom bestowed a cold, predatory scrutiny.

"Has Leonidas told you of the trouble in the Priory?" Brom quietly asked the boy.

The boy's voice was faint, hoarse. "Yes."

"What I ask of you is no simple task. Are you willing to do whatsoever may be required of you to resist mortal temptations and, if need be, to sacrifice your own life to vanquish the forces of darkness that now threaten humanity?"

This time Lorand's voice was stronger. "I am willing."

A low whisper crept from the dark lord's lips. "We shall see."

Brom studied the boy for a long time, causing Adrian to

become anxious. Then Brom said, "Your heart is true. Follow me... Alone." He glanced at Adrian and Leonidas. Noticing Leonidas' sputtering torch, Brom flicked two fingers in its direction. The torch immediately extinguished as if it had been plunged into a bucket of water. Only the whitish glare of the fog beyond the half-open door provided any illumination for the two older men as they peered into the depths of the darkness. "When he returns, he will be in deep meditation. Do not speak to him, for your words may break the trance."

"This is not wise," Adrian finally said. "I find it reprehensible to subject this boy to black magic."

"He will not harm the boy," Leonidas replied. Adrian felt the old man's eyes upon him. "He has much power, but he does not use it heedlessly."

"No. He uses it with much calculation." Adrian recalled Brom's remote, unearthly eyes. The monk knew that such a mind would not hesitate to sacrifice an innocent life if it were the most practical move to attain his goals.

After several minutes, Adrian suddenly seemed to discern movement in the grand hall leading away from the entryway. A slender shaft of moonlight illuminated the hooded figure of Lorand wandering silently toward the two older men. They stepped aside, looking in wonder as the boy passed them without a word and descended the stone steps of the Tower. A flock of ravens on the steps screeched and gave flight, disturbed by the boy's movement. He mounted his nervous horse and waited, hunched on the saddle.

Adrian and Leonidas followed and mounted their own steeds. The old man led the way down the mountain, and when they reached the crumbled ruins of the archway, Leonidas pointed out a path that meandered away to the south. "Follow this path to the river. There you will see another path that heads north along the edge of the forest. It will save you several hours' time. You will reach the Priory before dawn. My best wishes go out to you, my old friend. Take good care of the boy."

Leonidas was correct about the path; Adrian and Lorand reached the monastery grounds well before dawn. The familiar sight of the cathedral's stone spires rose ominously out of the diminishing fog, and around the weathered cathedral several humble, dilapidated stone and thatch buildings loomed like wounded ghosts. The Priory, his home for so many years, had once been a peaceful, cheering sight to him, but now the sagging stables devoid of their horses and the rectory with its darkened windows presented a grim, lifeless tableau. The entity stalking the Priory's halls had frightened away most of the livestock, and Adrian knew that behind each lightless window huddled one or more of the brothers, waiting out the night, praying and listening to the dark presence making its way through the buildings.

Carrying a torch, young Brother Vernon met Adrian and Lorand as they made their way to the stable. He helped them dismount and guide the horses to their stalls, his face somewhat cheerful as he informed Adrian that the night had passed quietly.

"We heard no disturbances," Vernon said. "The night passed without incident. Perhaps it has left us alone."

Adrian, stiff and irritable from the long ride through the mountains, responded curtly. "No," he scoffed, "I doubt it would oblige us so." He took the torch from the young monk, who hurried off to inform the others that Adrian had returned. Curious and concerned about Lorand's condition, Adrian turned to his silent companion, and in the torchlight he saw into the depths of the boy's cowl. To his dismay, instead of Lorand's wide, youthful eyes, he was met with Brom's searing, wolf-like gaze.

Adrian's breath caught in his throat. He wanted to recoil in horror, but he forced himself to stand his ground. "What is this deception?" he whispered fiercely.

"It was the only way," Brom replied. "I have risked much by coming here with you. No one must know that I have left the Tower." Brom cocked his head. The murmurs and footsteps of several brothers could be heard coming down the path to them. "I have no reason to mistrust you," Brom continued, "but there can be no room for trust in this mission. You will not leave my side, and you will tell no one of my true identity. Heed my words, for if you have any thoughts to betray me, you shall surely die before you can act upon them."

"I will not be threatened." Adrian's voice was thin and fearful.

"Then perhaps I should simply kill you to assure your silence."

Brom's eyes looked off to the eastern sky, which was lightening in preparation for dawn. Adrian sensed the barest hint of discomfort in the creature. As the other monks approached, Brom whispered, "Remember. Choose your words carefully."

"Brother Adrian," said Brother Dimitri in greeting. A tall, imposing figure with an imperious gait, the monk had seen more than seventy summers and was still as confident and strong as a horseman, although the events of recent days had etched lines of care on his rugged face. The other monks around him nodded in greeting to Adrian and his guest.

"Allow me to present Bertrand," Adrian said suddenly, invoking the name of his brother, who had perished in the Holy Land a generation ago. He glanced at Brom. "He is the emissary of the Lord of Vasaria."

Dimitri studied Brom, then looked back to the old monk. "Then your journey was a success?" Dimitri asked with some embarrassment. There was a suggestion of fear on the monk's face, and Adrian saw similar emotions on the countenances of the other brothers, emotions ranging from anxiety to disgust.

Adrian knew that sanctioning the aid of the unholy ruler of the Dark Tower offended and even horrified many of the brothers, but it had been a necessary decision and Adrian had taken it upon himself to put the future of the Priory in Brom's hands. Since the death of Abbot Firenza some months ago, Adrian had tacitly become the Priory's new leader, though no true election had taken place. He was by no means the eldest brother at St. Sebastian nor the most learned, but he suspected his unfortunate past as a soldier in the King's army had somehow turned him into a leader in the eyes of his brethren.

It was a weight he would have preferred not to carry, but in the current matter, his beloved Priory was in jeopardy. Action had to be taken.

"Bertrand will assist me with this matter," Adrian said. "He has been entrusted with the wisdom that we will require."

The monks once again turned their attention to Brom.

"Show me to the chapel," Brom said curtly. "I need to see the girl."

Brom and Adrian stood before the altar, as the low, rhythmic murmurs of the brothers chanting morning prayers came to them from the rectory. Since the murder of the girl and the desecration of the chapel, Adrian had sealed off the cathedral as if it were contaminated, and now the prayers were held in the rectory.

As the eastern sky lightened, the stained glass windows took on an unearthly red and blue glow that intensified with every passing minute. Brom gazed down at the empty altar and the blood-filled chalices encircling it.

"Where is she?" Brom asked.

Adrian gestured to an antechamber in the shadows beyond the altar. "In the abbot's private chamber. I thought it best to move her there rather than chance her father seeing such a horrific sight. Her father is a stablehand here. He often brings supplies here and frequently trades the Priory's vegetables and wines in the neighboring villages."

Brom studied the blood-filled goblets. "Did you not say that seven chalices surrounded the girl's body when it was discovered?"

Adrian's eyes fell upon the altar, counting only six silver goblets there. "I do not understand. I could not have been mistaken. There were three cups at each of her sides, and one above her head."

Brom scrutinized the stone floor running the length of the chapel. "Who else has been here?"

"No one could have entered the room. The cathedral was sealed after we discovered the body. I locked the doors myself and I carry the only key."

Brom took notice of a statue beside the altar depicting a man tied to a post. Seven arrows protruded from his body.

"Saint Sebastian," Adrian said, looking up at the grim sculpture, "the patron saint of our abbey. He was a martyr, sentenced to death for his faith. The Emperor's archers filled his body with arrows, but they could not kill him."

Brom returned his attention to the altar and lifted one of the goblets to his nose, inhaling its aroma as if it were a fine wine. Adrian's face betrayed the revulsion he felt.

Brom's eyes glittered briefly with something akin to amusement at the monk's unease. "This is not the girl's blood," he said.

"How do you know?"

Without answering, Brom strode over to the antechamber behind the altar and opened its heavy door. A narrow beam of dawning light broke through a gap in the velvet drapes, illuminating the pitiful sight of a crude pine coffin lying upon the abbot's immense oak reading table. Adrian lifted away the casket's lid, unleashing the nauseous, intensifying stench of putrefaction. Brom, however, appeared not to notice the fetid smell.

"Her name was Helena," Adrian said, the still-lovely face of the pale, dark-haired girl filling him with a sadness that was rapidly evolving, in some sort of emotional alchemy, into a furious rage. The poor girl was a year or two from becoming a woman, from venturing out into the world and making a life for herself. Now she was no more.

Brom studied the familiar sigil painted in blood on the girl's torso. It was as the monk had said—the same symbol that adorned the doors of the Dark Tower. The twisting flourishes and radiant spikes seemed to have been rendered by the skilled hand of an artist. The crimson rune appeared to be a component of the grisly ritual, but its significance remained unknown.

Brom ran his thin fingers down the girl's arms and legs, examining her unspoiled skin. A garland of lilies hung tightly about her throat. Brom's fingertips brushed the skin of her neck underneath the garland. "There are no cuts or punctures on her body. The blood in the chalices is not hers." To Adrian's skeptical look, Brom responded by lifting the girl's hand and swiping a claw across the discolored underside of the arm. Blood began to seep from the flesh.

"She has lost no blood at all," Adrian said in dismay. "If not hers, then whose blood fills those goblets?"

"It is not the blood of a human."

"How can you be certain?"

Brom's eyes narrowed. "Trust me when I tell you that I know the scent of human blood all too well." He lifted the girl's closed eyelids, revealing pupils that had become pools of scarlet.

Adrian made the sign of the cross while Brom gently

took hold of Helena's chin and moved her head from side to side. Something in the movement and the soft crackle of bone made the old monk furrow his brow in confusion. "Her neck has been broken."

"Yes. But why the ritual?" Brom seemed to be asking the question of himself. He noticed something lodged between the strands of her disheveled hair. His fingers plucked a withered leaf from her raven-black tresses.

Adrian peered closely at the leaf. "From an apple tree," he said.

Brom nodded, then turned to leave. "Her body must be blessed, then burned before another day passes. See to it."

Though Brom had instructed Adrian to draw the curtains in the rectory and the library, he could sense the arrival of daylight the way an animal can sense when it is being hunted. He stood at the hearth of the austere dining hall, his back to the table where Adrian sat with Brother Radovic, an earnest young man who was recounting his experience with the entity prowling the grounds of the Priory.

"It was two nights ago," Radovic said, "and I was sweeping up in the wine cellar. My thoughts were elsewhere, but then suddenly the cellar became unbearably cold. I felt a freezing chill, as if I had been submerged in an icy lake. I could see frost forming on the bottles. I called out to the brothers working in the kitchen above, but they did not answer. Instead..." The boy's voice trailed off.

"Go on," Adrian said gently.

"Instead, I felt a presence behind me. I thought it must be one of the brothers, but when I turned... I saw an immense shadow in the form of a man. It had no face, yet I could sense it gazing at me, looking deep into me. Like some bird of prey, the creature unfurled majestic black wings that rose like smoke from a torch. I cried out and fell to my knees in prayer, and the beast took flight, sailing over my head down the corridor, and as it streaked by the racks of wine, the bottles exploded, one after another, until the cellar was awash in a river of crimson."

Brom said nothing, his attention held by the crackling flames of the hearth.

"Thank you, Brother Radovic," Adrian said.

When the young monk excused himself, Adrian joined Brom at the fireplace. "You have heard a great deal, yet you have said very little."

Brom had indeed heard a great deal. Radovic's tale was merely one of numerous similar accounts related by the monks during the course of the morning. The tales ranged from ominous sensations of a watchful presence lurking in bedchambers at night to heavy footfalls echoing throughout the catacombs beneath the cathedral. Brother Laszlo reported seeing a glimpse of some hideous, skeletal fiend in his dressing mirror one morning, but like Radovic's entity, it quickly vanished. Not one of the monks had any knowledge of how the forbidden scroll had gone missing. The words of the brothers lingered in Brom's mind like discordant notes without a melody, fragments of a puzzle that seemed to defy an easy solution.

"Do you believe what the brothers have told you is the truth?" Adrian asked.

Brom regarded the monk with interest. "Such a question implies that perhaps you do not."

Adrian sighed and looked away, his careworn face haggard and tense. "One of our rank has stolen the forbidden scroll. That much is obvious. You have heard from everyone in the Priory, so it is clear that one of us is touched with guilt."

"If this scroll possessed such terrible power, why was it not destroyed?"

The old monk hesitated before speaking. "That," Adrian said wearily, "has been a source of much debate over the years. I bear much responsibility for its continued existence, I fear."

"How so?"

"The Church's history has not always been a holy, glorious one, Lord Brom. In the name of God, the Church has often eradicated the wisdom and teachings of other lands, other cultures. Branding all other beliefs as heresy, the Church burned the libraries at Alexandria and other cities.... I was adamant that we not suppress knowledge of any kind, even knowledge that may seem unpalatable. A thousand years hence, perhaps the Church may find itself at the point of a sword, just as the defenders of Alexandria found themselves. Would we want our teachings, the records of our divine wisdom, to be burned and forgotten?"

"Unfortunately, the wisdom of your decision seems to be much in doubt at present." Brom heard the rattling of a wagon beyond the rectory's walls.

"That will be Phillipe," Adrian said. "Helena's father."

In the catacombs beneath the cathedral, Brom, Adrian and Phillipe stood before the closed coffin in which Helena lay. Several other monks had gathered in a semicircle around the casket, chanting their soothing, consoling hymns of deliverance from the tribulations of the living.

Banish the darkness engulfing this child, O Lord,
that her soul may know eternal peace.
Lord of Everlasting Light, hear our prayer.
Let her spirit be reborn into your kingdom, O Lord,
that she may rejoice in your divine grace.
Lord of Everlasting Life, hear our prayer.

The stocky, rough-hewn Phillipe had shut his eyes tightly and his head was bowed as he fought off a wave of tears. His heavy, calloused hands, hardened by a lifetime of labor, trembled as they pressed themselves over his face. A strangled sob escaped his throat, and Adrian took his elbow and led him away from the casket to an alcove. Brom accompanied them.

"The soul of your daughter is now in the hands of God," Adrian said. "You must always remember that she is far more happy now than we who are left upon this world."

Phillipe nodded, his anguished eyes downcast and almost beyond consolation.

"Your pain is great," Brom said quietly, "but the need for justice now is greater. It is imperative that you tell us of the girl's final acts in the days leading to her death."

Phillipe cast a stricken look over his shoulder at the coffin silhouetted by candlelight. "My daughter often accompanied me when I made journeys to other villages in this region. She would help me trade the Priory's goods, and she would help me care for the Priory's horses. She was rarely out of my sight."

"She was a young girl," Brom said, "but did she have any lovers? Any admirers here or in other hamlets?"

Phillipe shook his head, tightly shutting his eyes again as a fresh wave of tears wracked his body.

"Any enemies?" Brom asked.

"No. She was a sweet girl and all loved her." Phillipe caught his breath and struggled to regain his composure. "Several days ago, though, Helena had become quite sad and withdrawn. I believe it was connected with a delivery of food we made last month to a small hamlet in the hills near Tyresia where many people had grown sick during the summer. After we returned from the village, I learned from the brothers that it had actually been stricken by plague and the Church had razed it, fearing the sickness would spread to other towns. I believe my daughter was haunted by this knowledge—by this glimpse of the punishing cruelty of the world." The man's eyes glinted with momentary hostility at Adrian.

"I do not defend the Church's actions," Adrian said. "My heart grieves for that village. All those with any humanity are shamed by what transpired."

Phillipe wandered back to the coffin of his daughter, where he knelt in prayer. The other monks closed ranks around him, continuing their hymn of deliverance.

Brom turned his attention to a fading mural in a dimly lit alcove. The painting depicted fierce, sword-wielding angels bedecked in gleaming armor as they clashed with grotesque but equally ferocious demons in a turbulent, apocalyptic wasteland littered with ruined castles and pools of fire. Brom silently stared at the mural for a long while, intently scrutinizing the age-worn details. His eyes searched for the artist's name among the intricate swirls of ancient paint but there was no signature to be found.

"Who painted this image?" Brom asked.

"I do not know," Adrian said. "This wall has been here since the monastery was first constructed." Like Brom, Adrian surveyed the painting, but without Brom's keen interest. "The warring angels are the Seraphim, God's chosen ones. They are the immortal guardians of the eternal kingdom." He narrowed his eyes. "Perhaps our attention would be better focused on the entity prowling these halls rather than discussing the history of the monastery's artwork."

"I have not forgotten my mission," Brom replied, keeping his eyes locked on the painting. "Look closely at the symbol on the armor."

Adrian squinted into the shadowy alcove. Upon the breastplate of one warrior angel was an emblem eerily reminiscent of the sigil emblazoned upon the door of the Dark Tower and in many other areas of Brom's accursed keep, as well as upon the body of the girl.

"There is more than one mystery to resolve here," Brom said, "and they are somehow linked together."

Adrian grew impatient. "You were summoned here to banish the evil that threatens our sanctuary. That is where our efforts need to be directed."

Brom's voice was calm. "I chose to come here for other reasons as well. Do not lecture me on the wisest course of action. It was not I that elected to keep the forbidden scroll in existence. If this sanctuary is in peril, it is your own doing."

Before Adrian could reply, Brother Radovic appeared breathlessly beside them, his face pale and troubled. "Brother Adrian, please—there has been another incident. In the library."

The circular, windowless library dominated the western end of the rectory, filled with thousands of scrolls and ancient tomes. Brom sensed that it had once been a quiet haven of learning and meditation, but the scene before him was now one of chaos and looming fear. Every scroll and volume rested in place, but the massive tables that once stood at the center of the room had been pushed aside and the rug beneath them had been rolled away. A strange message, etched in the flagstones, circled round the engraved image of a tree in the middle of the floor, under the building's dome. The chiseled letters and central design were filled with a dark red liquid that appeared to be blood.

Several monks hovered in the doorway, afraid to enter. Brother Dimitri grimly crossed himself. "Almighty Savior," he whispered.

"The hand of God had no part in this," Adrian remarked, wandering into the library and circling the macabre inscription.

"I came here a short while ago to retrieve a volume of Scripture," young Radovic said, "and the library was in perfect order. As I passed this way a few moments later, I discovered this." The young monk gestured a trembling hand toward the floor. "I saw no one else in the hall."

Adrian surveyed the rest of the room while Brom studied the cryptic message.

Crouching, Brom ran his hand along the crimson letters and brought his bloodstained fingers beneath his nose. "Animal's blood," he said, "the same blood that filled the chalices." As his eyes followed the winding words, he read the phrase aloud. "Arbore di Sapientia est radix en scientia quod veritas."

"The inscription is Latin," Adrian said, "perhaps centuries old." He stepped to Brom's side and translated the words. "The Tree of Wisdom is rooted in knowledge and truth."

"Another clue from our mysterious spirit," Brom said quietly.

A look of bewilderment settled over Adrian's face. "But how could it have known this ancient inscription was here, beneath the rug? In all my years, we have never discovered it."

Brom stepped across the threshold of crimson letters. A withered leaf rested on the floor at the center of the tree design. He picked the leaf up and turned it about between his fingers.

Adrian stood at his shoulder. "Another apple tree leaf?"

"Yes," Brom replied, remembering the leaf he had discovered in the dead girl's hair. "Is there an orchard on the Priory's grounds?"

"Yes," Adrian said, "beyond the cathedral. Why?"

"You will need to search among the trees and look for anything unusual. I cannot venture beyond the monastery's walls while daylight still reigns."

"I will go nowhere until you tell me your thoughts."

Brom understood the monk's frustration and ignored the harshness of his tone. "The blood in the chalices was lamb's blood. According to many beliefs, such an offering can cleanse the soul of unbaptized innocents who die as infants."

Adrian's confusion was evident. "Then the girl was not the subject of some unholy sacrifice?"

"Go to the orchard," Brom said. "If my suspicions are correct, you will find your answer there."

In the catacombs, Brom considered the mural of warring angels and the diabolical army while he awaited Adrian's return. A pair of candles lit the alcove with meager, flickering light, and the shimmering firelight seemed to animate the painted figures. Was the painting a depiction of the Great War in Heaven many eons in the past, or was it some prophetic vision of events yet to come?

He sensed Adrian's presence before the monk had even drawn near. "You have found something," Brom said.

Adrian appeared at his side, a tattered length of rope in his hand. One end was frayed as if it had been cut with a rough knife. "It was knotted around a branch in the deepest reaches of the orchard." Adrian shook his head, unable to accept what the evidence suggested. "This makes no sense."

Brom's stern gaze softened. "Do not let your heart blind you from the truth, Brother Adrian."

As the monk silently studied the coil of rope, a dismal sadness clouded his eyes.

"Bring me Phillipe," Brom said quietly.

In the abbot's private chambers, Phillipe stood by the heavily draped casement window as if peering out into the world beyond. Like a phantom, Brom stood in a shadowy corner, mindful of the slender, almost negligible blade of gray daylight that spilled from between the halves of the curtains.

"She was already dead when I found her hanging from the

tree," Phillipe said, his voice little more than a ruined whisper. "My beautiful daughter. My heart is lost without her..."

"You must tell us what happened," Adrian urged.

"The day before her death," Phillipe said, "she confessed to me she was afraid she had brought back the plague from the hamlet I had sent her to. She had been feeling sick... She was terrified she would bring the pestilence to our village. My darling girl, she was always so fearful, so fanciful in her imaginings, very much like her mother... I chided her for causing herself unnecessary anguish. 'You are as healthy as I am,' I told her. It was the last thing I said to her and I now regret my foolish words. The following day, I found her in the orchard. That day, my soul itself perished, for I could not bear to think of my beautiful daughter taking her own life and consigning herself to Hell." Tears coursed down his hollow cheeks.

"You are the one responsible for the theft of the scroll," Adrian said. "Is it not so?"

Phillipe nodded but said nothing.

"But it defies reason," Adrian said. "No one but a select few of the brothers knew of the scroll's existence, so how would you come to learn of it? And the scroll's foul contents have resisted even the most intensive efforts of our scholars, so why would you have need for such an arcane object?"

"He did not act alone," Brom said quietly, gazing at the sorrowful father. "Is that not true?"

Phillipe drew in a weary breath before he could summon his voice. "Ever since Helena was a small girl and began to visit the monastery with me she spoke of a mysterious dark monk who had befriended her. She spent time in the catacombs and although she said she was with him, no one else ever saw him. I assumed he was not real, a creation of a lonely child's imagination. She called him Brother Talos.

"After I cut Helena down from the tree, I was wracked with torment, praying to the Lord to spare my daughter from the fires of damnation. Brother Talos came to me as if in answer to my prayers. His kindness shone from his eyes like an inner fire. He told me there was a way to save her soul and ensure her everlasting life at the throne of the Almighty, but the secret lay in a scroll within the Priory's walls. While the brothers slept, I crept into the library and stole the scroll and brought it to Brother Talos in the cathedral along with the body of Helena.

"Brother Talos then instructed me to sacrifice a female lamb upon the altar and drain its blood into seven chalices. He appeared to slip into a trance as he prayed over my beloved girl. I did not understand his invocation, for his voice was low and the words sounded ancient. He bade me to offer my own prayer before the statue of Saint Sebastian, to protect the Priory from the plague. He then traced a strange symbol on my daughter's body using the lamb's blood. When he was done, he told me that the fate of my daughter's soul rested in the hands of the Almighty.

"Daylight was fast upon us, and we heard the brothers stirring in the rectory, and Brother Talos told me to drape a garland around Helena's neck to conceal the bruises from the rope so the brothers would not see the truth. I had no time to remove her body from the cathedral...." Once more, tears interrupted his speech. "I would surrender my life in a moment if I could be assured that my daughter's soul reposes in the Heaven that she deserves."

"She does," Brom said. "Of that I am certain. I know the plague well; many years ago did I see its dark passage through these lands. Though she did not yet bear the lesions of plague, the blood in her eyes was an omen of its deadly presence within her. She sacrificed herself rather than bring certain death to others.

In Scripture such an act is rewarded with the gift of Paradise."

Phillipe looked searchingly at Brom. "With all my heart, I hope your words are true. My own soul, however, is damned. With that scroll I have unleashed some vile evil within the Priory's walls."

"You are not damned," Adrian replied, "for your actions were motivated by the purest of loves. The scroll brought forth no diabolical scourge." The monk embraced the sorrowful man and led him out of the chamber.

When Adrian returned, Brom asked, "What do you know of this mysterious Brother Talos?"

"There is no Brother Talos here," Adrian said. "I have not heard his name before this day, and yet it seems he has been with us for quite some time. Perhaps he lived and died here long ago and his spirit has returned to haunt these halls."

"Perhaps." Brom's eyes darted around the dim chamber surveying the shadows for unseen phantoms. "Whatever he is, he is at the center of this mystery."

"Yes," Adrian replied. "It seems he left a trail of clues for us to follow, but why?"

Brom cast his gaze upon the shimmering flame of the room's lone candle. "I feel he has something yet to tell us."

While Adrian and several other monks prepared to hold a mass for Helena's soul in the cathedral, Brom returned to the catacombs. The sound of chanting filled the subterranean chamber with mournful echoes. He thought of Helena, but the tragedy of her life receded as he stood once more before the ancient mural depicting the war in Heaven. Since the moment he first discovered the painting, the image had loomed with mystical portent in his mind. As he studied the intricate details of the composition, his eyes fell upon a detail he had not noticed before. A crimson arrow between two clashing figures seemed to have been recently added. Brom inspected the arrow closely, verifying his suspicions that it too had been painted with lamb's blood. Following the arrow's tip, his eyes came to rest upon the entrance to a narrow passage hidden in shadows.

Entering the passageway, Brom discovered a shallow stone staircase leading down to a tunnel chiseled into the earth. Recessed niches filled with human bones lined the walls of the corridor, displaying the final resting places of the Priory's ancient dead. After a short distance, the tunnel branched into three separate paths. Noticing another arrow painted in blood, Brom followed the path it designated. Each time he came to a new branch, Brom discovered another arrow, and each time he allowed the crimson marker to guide his way. The low murmur of the monk's chants fell silent as he wound further into the darkness. Though not as vast as the labyrinth beneath the Dark Tower, the Priory's catacombs presented ample confusion for unwary explorers. The trail of arrows, however, brought Brom swiftly to his destination.

At last he came to an oaken door, deep in the heart of the maze. Brom laid a firm hand upon the knotted wood and the heavy door swung open, revealing an ornate vaulted chamber. Warily he entered the room, discovering a lavish collection of art and literature hidden far beneath the monastery. Hundreds of scrolls and ancient books rested on shelves, untouched by the ravages of time. At the center of the room, a solitary candle rested on a large desk filled with mystical diagrams and leather-bound tomes.

One wall was decorated with a swirling, colorful mosaic of a grand tower being torn asunder by the fiery hand of God. The sight chilled Brom, though he knew it was most likely an image of the mythical Tower of Babel.

A voice emanated from the shadows at the far end of the

room. "Even the mightiest works of man are subject to the will of the Divine One, it is said." A figure cloaked in black sat motionless in the darkness upon a chiseled throne. The pale fingers of his hand delicately stroked the missing chalice.

Brom took a step closer. "Or perhaps merely a fable to frighten man into bowing before the will of the Church."

"I assure you that is not so," the dark monk said. "I saw that tower fall, in a fury of lightning and smoke. It felt as if the earth itself had been cleaved in two."

Brom stared at the cloaked figure. "Brother Talos."

The shadow lifted its hooded head, the faint trace of a smile upon his smooth, pale features.

"Why do you haunt this place, spirit?"

The dark monk rose from his seat, moving to the edge of the desk. He placed the silver goblet beside the flickering candle and the flame's glow revealed the chalice was now empty. "I am no more spirit than you, Lord Brom."

Brom's heart grew heavy with unease when he heard the shadow speak his name. "What is your purpose here?"

"I have walked these halls, for generation upon generation, but those around me failed to notice my presence. Their limited minds saw only darkness in the shadows. The innocent, accepting mind of Helena, however, saw the truth. After the ritual with that poor girl, the minds of the brothers were opened to the existence of the shadow realm, but still their prejudices distorted their vision. They chose to think of me as a vile phantom, a monster—and that is what they saw." He placed his pale hand upon the pages of an ancient book lying on the desk before him. An etching on the page depicted a radiant angel, but as he turned the book to face Brom, the image appeared to change to that of a fierce winged devil. "Man sees what he wishes to see, at the mercy of his own superstitions and fears."

"What are you, truly? Angel or demon?"

"There is little difference. We are all brethren. The old ones called us the Watchers." As Talos spoke, an ancient sadness passed over his face and a strange light seemed to burn within the creature's eyes, but Brom suspected it was merely the work of his own imagination. "In the fall from Heaven, I and others were caught between the warring factions. Angels clashed with their brethren in a struggle for supremacy that is still unfinished. Though many of us remained neutral, all of us have some burden of pain that we shall forever carry.

"You ask why I haunt this Priory. Many centuries ago, this fortress was no sanctuary for men of God. It was the stronghold of Prince Valkonour, the feared warrior who ruled these lands like a vengeful wraith for a lifetime. His only daughter, Iliana, was as celestially beautiful as her father was fierce. So beautiful and so angelically kind that she could even tempt a Watcher to fall before her on bended knee, in love and devotion."

Talos' expression of weariness and regret was strangely familiar to Brom; he suspected his own face bore the indelible ravages of such feelings. "I shared my gifts and my affection with her, and it resulted in the Prince setting her ablaze as a heretic and a servant of darkness. Since that day, my penance has been to isolate myself in this place so that I may never forget what I have wrought. Though I avoid the denizens of this monastery, I saw within Helena the same unearthly gentleness that I saw within Iliana. To that girl and to her father, I owed the deliverance of her wounded soul."

"Your penance appears more like damnation," Brom said.

"As does yours, Lord Brom." Talos' keen eyes peered deeply into Brom's own, and for the briefest moment Brom saw the Watcher as he must have appeared during the War in Heaven. Within the humble cowl, Talos' face shone with majestic beauty, more awe-inspiring than any ancient sculpture of Greek gods and mortal warriors. In a moment, however, the Watcher had resumed his more mundane disguise. "I know of your penance," Talos said softly, "and what you have sacrificed. You seek redemption. We are much the same, you and I."

"I am no celestial warrior."

"Not yet," the Watcher replied.

"You speak of me as though you know my fate. If so, speak plainly and prove to me you are more than a mere trickster spirit."

Talos considered Brom's challenging words, and a faint smile touched the Watcher's lips. "You are vital to the Master's plan, but you must discover your fate on your own. You are part of a great prophecy."

"What prophecy?"

"The prophecy of the Seraphim." From the depths of his robe, Talos produced a tattered scroll and presented it to Brom. The parchment was torn in places, and much of the ancient text was illegible.

"It is the scroll of Enoch," Talos explained. "Our tale is chronicled herein. The brothers here wrongly assumed it is a tool of blasphemy and evil, but in truth, it is the decree of the Almighty. It is the fulfillment of His Will, for among this scroll's secrets is a prophecy that the Seraphim shall inhabit and hold dominion over the earth."

"And what of man?"

Talos said nothing.

"I will have no part in mankind's destruction," Brom declared.

"You cannot escape your own destiny. Your only choice lies in the course you take."

A half-obscured symbol near the bottom of the parchment caught Brom's eyes. The symbol closely resembled the icon now so familiar to Brom during his isolation in the Dark Tower. "This sigil drew me here," Brom said at last.

"Yes, as it was intended to. We are truly but pawns in the Master's plan." Thoughtfully, the entity circled the large desk piled with books and scrolls. "It is the sign of the Seraphim, the icon of the Dark Tower. It is also a crucial component of the ritual that sanctified the soul of the young girl and assured her of life everlasting." He spoke wonderingly, as if much of the scroll's wisdom perhaps eluded his own mind. Yet Brom knew the ancient creature possessed considerable knowledge, much of it concerning Brom's own fate.

Brom gazed at the tattered scroll and the faded, ghostly ciphers of the several ancient languages that ran through the document as if it were the crossroads where the world's philosophies united.

"Can you tell me nothing more?"

The Watcher stared at him for a long moment. "I can tell you that your destiny will take you to Castle Rankorr, the stronghold of the Brotherhood of the Black Dawn. Therein lies a final truth that you must discover. Seek your answers there."

Talos held forth the silver chalice, but it was no longer empty. Brom stared into the pool of crimson that filled the goblet and was immediately enticed by the irresistible aroma that wafted from it. This was not lamb's blood, nor the blood of any mere mortal. Brom noticed a gaping slash across Talos' wrist, and a bloodstained dagger clenched firmly in his other hand.

"I know the essence of your life force, Lord Brom. I know how you have long resisted the temptation to quench your maddening thirst. If you dare travel to Castle Rankorr, you will need all your strength to face what awaits you there. This is my gift to you." He set the chalice down on the desk before Brom, and Brom could see that the wound on the Watcher's wrist was no more.

Brom stared at the chalice, straining to resist the dark desires that welled deep within him. "And what of my mission in the Dark Tower?"

"All things have their time, Lord Brom, and the time is not yet ripe for you to know. A sword's blade must be tempered in fire before it is ready for the field of battle. The truth of your path must be uncovered by you and no one else."

Again Brom's eyes searched the fragmented scroll, looking for the order behind the jumbled disorder of chaotic symbols and tantalizingly familiar phrases. When he looked up again, Brother Talos was gone and Brom was alone in the chamber.

The blazing colors of the cathedral's stained glass windows had gradually extinguished with the setting sun, and now the chapel was in virtual darkness as Brom stood before the altar, the scroll in his cloak and the Watcher's words echoing in his mind.

He heard Adrian approach from behind him. "The carriage you requested is out by the stables."

Brom nodded.

"What of Brother Talos?" Adrian asked. "Will the Priory still be haunted by his dark spirit?"

"It never was." Brom tersely explained what the entity had told him. "He will continue to walk these halls as he always has, but the brothers will no longer sense his presence if you tell them the evil has been banished. Man is quite susceptible to suggestion. We often see what we wish to see."

Brom reached beneath his cloak. "This should be returned to the tabernacle," he said, holding forth the missing chalice.

As Adrian took the empty goblet, he noticed a rekindled vitality in Brom's eyes. "And the scroll? What of its fate?"

Brom looked at the monk. "Lost."

There was perceptible relief in Adrian's eyes. "Perhaps that is for the best."

"Perhaps."

Brom stepped out of the cathedral into the chill night air and saw the dark carriage awaiting him.

Adrian spoke again, conveying a tone of heartfelt respect. "I know what you have risked by coming here, and you have my gratitude for all you have done. I hope you have found what you were seeking here as well."

"I have," Brom replied, "but there is still much left to discover."

"May you find the answers and the peace you seek, Lord Brom. And perhaps one day our paths will cross again."

Brom glanced at the monk. "Perhaps." He stepped into the carriage and asked the driver if he knew the way to Castle Rankorr.

The driver informed him that is was half a day's ride to the East.

"Take me there," Brom said.

Night of The Wolf

Joseph Vargo and Joseph Iorillo

The harvest moon shone bright and full, bathing the dense mountain woodlands in pale auburn light. Squinting to find his way in the gloom, Leonidas stepped warily over the twisted roots that covered the forest path as ravens watched in silence from the barren branches overhead. Ghostly shadows fluttered and closed in around him, encircling the old man like a legion of wraiths, and as he peered into the darkness between the surrounding trees, he caught the gleam of yellow eyes staring back. The eerie silence of the forest gave way to a low, guttural growl emanating from the blackness ahead. Leonidas stopped and stood as still as possible as a large form emerged from the shadows before him. The dark figure lumbered forth like a great hulking beast, then stood upright on its hind legs as it stepped closer. The creature stood a full head taller than the old man, its black form silhouetted against the rising moon. The ravens began to caw, filling the woods with a chorus of ghastly croaking. The black beast reached out with a clawed hand and grabbed the old man by the throat, lifting him off his feet and drawing him near. Leonidas struggled in vain and gasped for breath as the shadow's yellow eyes changed to a seething red glow.

Leonidas awoke from his dream, his aged heart pounding in his chest. The first rays of dawn broke through his window shutters, illuminating his small house with the welcome glow of daylight. Though he was safe in his home, the monstrous vision from his nightmare lingered to plague his mind. He hurriedly dressed and walked to the house across the road to share his concerns with Talik, the head of the council of elders.

Talik's face bore the scars of his youthful days as a mercenary, and his calloused hands looked as if they had been chiseled from stone. He put a mug of steaming broth in front of Leonidas and took a seat across the table. He listened in silence as his friend related his disturbing vision.

"It was just a dream," Talik reassured him, "brought on by the sounds of the howling wind during the storm last night."

"And if it was not?" Leonidas took a short sip from the mug in his hands. "You have known me all my life. I pay little heed to my dreams. But this—this was no mere nightmare."

Talik stared hard into his old friend's eyes. "Perhaps it was an omen." He began to speak again, but his words were interrupted by a quiet knock at his door. Talik rose from his seat and opened the door to see a village woman and her son standing outside. The young boy was pale and trembling, and his frayed cloak was damp in places. Talik invited them in, then sat by the fire. Although the hovel was warm, the boy's hands shook uncontrollably.

The frail woman leaned down close to her son's ear and whispered. "Do not be afraid. Tell them what you saw."

The boy stared at the floor and cleared his throat. "I was gathering firewood... just after dawn." His young voice quavered as he spoke. "I ventured further into the forest than I should have, and before I knew it, I had lost sight of the path. I came to the edge of a stream and was about to turn back when I heard a growling sound from the other side. Then I saw something moving beyond the trees, across the creek near the old gypsy camp."

Leonidas shifted his gaze to Talik, but the old man's stern face betrayed no sign of alarm.

"A wolf larger than any I have ever seen before crept from the shadows of the forest," the boy said. "It stood at the water's edge and bared its fangs at me. A moment later, two more were by its side."

Tears welled in the boy's eyes as he paused to clear his throat once more. "If the stream had not been swollen from the rain, they would have set upon me and torn me to pieces. I dropped my firewood and ran and did not stop until I reached the village."

"You are fortunate to return unharmed," Talik said. "Remember this lesson the next time you are tempted to stray from the forest path."

The boy nodded, then spoke again. "When I returned, I told my tale to my uncle. He said I saw the Volkodlak. He said he heard them howling in the night and saw their shadows lurking in the forest."

A look of concern crossed Leonidas's face, but before he could say a word, Talik rose to his feet and spoke again. "He meant only to frighten you for wandering off alone. There is no need to fear such monsters. We are safe in the village."

Talik nodded his head discreetly at the door. Leonidas sent the boy and his mother home, then followed his friend outside into the morning's autumn chill. The two men found themselves scanning the rough dirt tracks of Vasaria's few roads and the scattering of homes and stables that comprised the village. The surrounding forest seemed quiet and still, but Leonidas felt uneasy all the same. He could not escape the feeling that some insidious entity was lurking in the depths of the forest, watching him from the shadows, biding its time.

Talik's expression was grim. "We must separate fact from rumor to uncover the truth behind these stories."

"The boy's uncle is a drunken fool. Talking to him will do little good." Leonidas shook his head in disgust. "I will go to the old gypsy camp to see what I can find."

"Falon will accompany you."

Leonidas nodded his approval, knowing well that Talik's son, Falon, was the best hunter in Vasaria.

Talik turned his attention back toward the village. "The children should be kept indoors until we can resolve this problem. Tonight we must set traps and torches around the edge of the forest and alert the men to guard their stables."

Leonidas scanned the tree line until his eyes found the Dark Tower, barely visible in the early morning mist. "And what if these creatures are not mere wolves?"

"The Lord of the Tower will protect us... as he always has."

Leonidas remained silent, still studying the Tower. He turned to go back into his home but Talik clutched at his sleeve.

"Two nights ago you traveled there," the old man said, glancing at the Tower, "with young Lorand. Yet you have not spoken of it since. Is there anything you wish to tell me?"

Leonidas solemnly gazed into his friend's eyes. "Lord Brom is ever vigilant. As long as he watches over Vasaria, no harm will come to us."

Talik did not appear fully satisfied with the answer but he released his friend's arm.

Leonidas quickly returned home and unlocked a large oak chest to retrieve a long dagger, a bow of sturdy birch and a quiver of arrows. Though he was well into his sixth decade of life and only half as strong as he used to be, he was able to draw back the bowstring and hold it steady without too much pain.

Wasting little time, Leonidas made his way to the edge of the village where Falon stood waiting. Talik's son was lean and well-muscled, just as his father had been twenty years ago. A large bow and full quiver were slung across his back and several knives were tucked into his belt. The two silently ventured out into the woods, following the path the boy had taken to fetch firewood.

The morning mist hung heavy, obscuring the forest in an eerie haze. The creek where the boy encountered the wolf pack was but a short distance from the forest path to the east of the village. A fallen tree allowed the two men to cross the rushing stream safely. Once across, they followed the creek bank for a short while and soon came to a clearing where an overgrown circle of stones surrounded a large fire pit.

Leonidas recalled the place from his youth. "Years ago, a clan of gypsies settled in the forest. They made their camp here."

Surveying the abandoned campsite, Falon noticed the remnants of a rotted caravan wagon beneath a clump of tangled vines. "What became of them?"

"One night, at the end of the summer, they left without warning."

"They never returned?"

"No," the old man said quietly, a hint of sadness in his voice. "No one ever saw them again."

Leonidas circled the fire pit, stopping before a mossy boulder covered with strange markings. A ring of cryptic symbols was etched in the stone, surrounding an inverted star with five points and a crude carving of a wolf. The old man stared at the gypsy sigils, silently contemplating their meaning.

After a few moments, Falon asked, "What do you know of the Volkodlak?"

Leonidas furrowed his brow. "Where did you hear of such a thing?"

Falon smiled. "You know how quickly rumors sweep through our village."

"They are creatures from tales of long ago," Leonidas replied abruptly, trying to dismiss the topic.

"I have heard they are the Devil's minions, summoned forth by black magic—demons who roam the night as fierce, stalking beasts."

"If the legends are to be believed, they are unholy creatures of darkness—wampior who take the form of wolves beneath the light of the moon." Leonidas scanned the misty woods. "But as I have said, these are tales of long ago."

A sudden rustling of fallen leaves alerted them that something was prowling nearby. The two men stood silent and still, peering into the depths of the forest, but the encompassing mist obscured their view beyond a few yards. Falon crept quietly forward, then crouched to examine the ground in front of him, taking notice of a shallow impression in the muddy earth and leaves. The young hunter traced his finger around the shape, allowing Leonidas to see the outline of a large paw print.

Falon pointed to the ground ahead where a trail of similar tracks led off toward the creek bank. "Wait here," he whispered, then quickly disappeared into the fog following the trail.

The misty woods fell deathly silent and the sensation of being watched crept over Leonidas once more, sending an icy chill down his spine. Ever so slowly, he turned to look behind him and as he did, his eyes met the gleaming yellow gaze of a large timber wolf standing at the far edge of the clearing. Leonidas watched in horror as several other ghostly grey forms slowly emerged from the mist-shrouded woods, appearing like phantoms behind the fearsome beast. The wolf pack waited just beyond the treeline as the first wolf crept forward.

Leonidas' breath became shallow and labored, and he fought to control a surge of panic. He did not take his eyes off the advancing wolf as his hands slowly placed an arrow across his bow. The creature's eyes narrowed as it heard the creak of the bowstring drawing back. The arrow was aimed downward, and as Leonidas slowly raised it, the wolf emitted a low growl, then snarled, revealing its jagged fangs.

Leonidas released the arrow. It hissed through the air with lightning speed but narrowly missed its target, grazing the tip of the wolf's ear as it sailed over the creature's head. The snarling beast lunged forward and Leonidas staggered back, dropping his bow as he fumbled for the dagger in his belt. The wolf bounded across the clearing in two strides and leapt toward the old man, then the hiss of another arrow split the morning air.

Falon's arrow found its mark in the wolf's heart. With a yelp, the great beast dropped to the ground, crashing into the mud a few feet before Leonidas. The animal's jaws snapped mindlessly at the air and then its yellow eyes lost their seething intensity, becoming finally glassy and dull with death.

Falon stalked forward, shouting and brandishing a long dagger, scattering the other wolves away. The young hunter crouched beside Leonidas to examine the fallen beast. The boy's description had not been exaggerated. From snout to hindquarters, the creature was larger than even a good-sized man. Leonidas laid a hand upon the blood-soaked fur over the wolf's stilled heart. As ferocious as the creature appeared, it did not match the horrific monster from his dream. "These creatures are not unholy beasts," Leonidas murmured, "they are merely wolves."

"How can you be certain?"

Leonidas looked upward at the dim light penetrating the forest canopy. "Creatures of darkness cannot withstand the rays of the sun. They could not roam freely in the light of day."

"Something has driven them from their usual hunting grounds near the caverns," Falon said, sheathing his dagger.

"It would seem so." Leonidas squinted at the retreating wolves as they receded into the forest mist.

"But what could cause them to flee their lair?"

"Perhaps a wildfire, or a flood. Perhaps a larger predator. We must determine the cause of this before night falls."

As they turned to leave, Leonidas' eyes fell upon the boulder engraved with gypsy sigils once again. The mossy stone was spattered with the dead wolf's blood, staining the pagan inscription dark red.

Much of the morning fog dissolved away as the hunters returned to Vasaria. At the edge of the village, Leonidas turned to Falon. "Tell your father to assemble the elder council. I will meet with them shortly. I must do something first."

Over the generations, Vasaria's hunters had been diligent in ridding the surrounding forest of wolves. It had been many years since the lethal creatures had dared bother the village, and yet suddenly they had returned, with a boldness that he found unsettling. If dark forces were indeed at work, there was one person in Vasaria who might offer insight.

At the southern edge of the village sat Daria's small

abode. The grey smoke from her chimney filled the air with a strangely alluring aroma that put a smile on Leonidas' troubled face. The woman sustained herself by mending clothes and tending to the sick and dying with her mystical herbs and poultices, but the elders of Vasaria often called upon her in times of trouble, for they knew she had the gift of prophecy.

As Leonidas sat with her by the fire, however, she smiled gently and shook her head. "You are seven summers too late," she said. "Before my daughter was born, I possessed the gift of second sight. The spirits would speak to me through tea leaves and bones to tell me of destiny's plans. Once little Annika was born, though, the spirits fell silent, and the gift was lost, just as it was with my mother before me."

Daria could see the disappointment in the old man's eyes. "What is it that makes you so anxious for prophecy?"

Leonidas averted his gaze, his face softening into an expression of weariness and embarrassment. "Perhaps it is just an old man's irrational fear. The wolves of the forest have grown restless and have left their hunting grounds in the valley."

"Surely we are protected within the village."

"Yes."

"But something else troubles you."

"Last night I dreamt of a great black beast with burning eyes. It resembled a monstrous wolf, but it walked upright like a man."

"The Volkodlak?"

"There is no need to start rumors before we are sure of the facts."

"No," Daria acknowledged, "but there is no harm in preparing for the worst." She opened a tall cabinet beside her stove and began searching through the numerous earthen jars that lined the shelves. After a few moments, she withdrew some dried leaves and flower petals and began to crush them beneath her pestle. "Wolfsbane will protect you," she said. "The slightest touch of it is poisonous to these beasts." When she had ground the leaves to a fine powder, she poured it into a small leather pouch and handed it to Leonidas. "Let us hope you need not use it."

"Let us hope." He squeezed her hand in gratitude.

Leonidas stepped out into the cold, overcast day and surveyed his surroundings, his eyes lingering on the darkness at the tree line. Noticing little Annika sitting in a patch of earth beside the doorway, Leonidas crouched and laid a hand on the girl's head.

"It will not be safe to be outside this evening," he said. "The forest is filled with unwelcome visitors." Leonidas took notice of the jumble of whitened bone fragments the girl was shuffling in her small hands.

The girl cupped her hands together and shook the bones, then solemnly tossed them into a circle traced in the dirt in front of her. The grim tokens landed in a strange pattern and Annika leaned in close to study them. As she did, Leonidas noticed that the skeletal fragments were adorned with carvings of mystical symbols and ancient runes.

"Ravens," the girl said quietly. "And wolves. They will share the forest tonight." She carefully gathered up the bits of bones and looked up at him. "This is a sign of great danger."

Remembering his dream, Leonidas cast a scrutinizing gaze over the girl. "What else do you see, young one?"

Annika shut her eyes and threw the skeletal runes again, then opened her eyes and stared intently into the ring of bones. "Darkness looms on the horizon," she said. "Beware the rise of the black dawn."

"And the wolves? What more can you tell me about them?"

The girl looked at him and gathered up the bones. Once again she cast them into the circle. "The white wolf has returned to claim the Tower as its own."

"How can this be?"

Annika snatched up the bones and with another flick of her wrist sent the ivory fragments into the dirt one final time. "The keep stands unguarded."

Leonidas was startled to see the white bones form the strange sigil emblazoned upon the Dark Tower's door. The sigil, however, appeared to be broken in half like a shattered sword. He stood up and stared off at the Tower on the mountain, partially obscured by a lingering veil of mist. His hands trembled as he recalled the events that had transpired on his last visit to the Tower and a grim realization set in. Without another word, he hurried away to the council of elders.

Talik's modest hovel was crowded with the gathering of village elders. The venerable council was in the midst of discussion, but the room fell silent and all eyes turned to Leonidas as he entered.

Talik rose from his chair near the flickering hearth. "Falon has told us of the troubles in the forest. The wolves must be driven back to their hunting grounds."

Leonidas stepped to the center of the room. "I fear our troubles may stretch beyond this plague of wolves."

The others gazed at him questioningly.

"I have borne witness to omens of great evil. A grim prophecy is unfolding."

The grave tone of his voice drew Talik's concern. "What is this prophecy?"

"Darkness draws near Vasaria," Leonidas replied. "For

centuries it has waited, longing to return to the Tower where it dwelled long ago."

"How can you be certain of this?" asked Gonrath, the elder scribe.

"I have seen the signs," Leonidas said. "The prophecy warns us to beware the rise of the black dawn and foretells the return of the white wolf."

A look of dread swept over Gonrath's face. "Lord Brom will surely protect us, will he not?"

"He cannot help us," Leonidas said.

Talik narrowed his eyes at his friend. "Why?"

Leonidas had difficulty meeting the older man's gaze. "I fear he has left the Tower."

The room erupted in murmurs of disbelief and outrage.

Talik pounded his staff against the floor to quiet the crowd. "This cannot be. Where has he gone? The Tower cannot be left unguarded!" The firelight cast menacing shadows across his weathered features. "Leonidas, what transpired when you took Lorand at the Tower? Now is not the time for secrets."

"No, it is not," Leonidas said, "but the truth has been covered in shadows." The old man paused to take a deep breath. "I believe Lord Brom has gone to the Monastery of St. Sebastian to aid them with their plight. He left the boy Lorand in his place, to stand guard over the keep until he has returned. To ensure complete secrecy, he trusted no one with his plan. Even I was unaware."

The white-bearded Kasmarak rose to his feet, a look of terror in his eyes. "He has forsaken us!"

"No," Leonidas replied firmly. "Lord Brom understands the dire importance of his vigil, perhaps better than anyone ever has, but he has yet to unlock all of the Tower's mysteries.

He has studied the Baron's journals and explored the depths of the catacombs beneath the keep, and though he has discovered much, many secrets still remain beyond his grasp. He has ventured to the monastery to seek answers—answers that will allow him to fulfill his own destiny to vanquish the darkness imprisoned within the Tower."

Talik stood silent for a long moment as he pondered his friend's words. The weight of the situation bore down on him like a cauldron of burning coals, but his face revealed no hint of panic or fear. At last he addressed the waiting council. "We have lived our entire lives in the shadow of the Tower. We have chronicled its dark history and passed the tales on to our children, yet there is much that remains hidden, even to us. We have never truly known the ways of the Dark Lord, only that he protects us and keeps vigil over the Tower. We do not question his motives—we merely have faith in his wisdom, and our faith has kept us safe for nine generations.

"We now face a dark nemesis that threatens us all. Until Lord Brom returns, we must deal with this matter on our own, as best we can."

Leonidas stepped to Talik's side then turned to face the council. "We must take heed of the prophecy. The white wolf draws near." He scanned the somber faces around him, staring deep into each man's eyes. "You know of whom I speak. His name is chronicled in the ebon scrolls, as is the prophecy of the Black Dawn. He is the last remaining servant of Queen Mara."

Gonrath, being well-versed in the legends of the Tower, spoke out in disbelief. "This cannot be. The one you speak of is dead, slain by the Baron's own hand during Mara's fall."

"No," Leonidas said. "He did not perish. Somehow he has survived the long years, and he now seeks to gain dominion over the Tower. If he is not stopped, the Dark Queen will rise again. We cannot allow this to happen."

Talik cast a stern look around the room, the reflection of firelight burning in his eyes. "We have dealt with wolves before. We know their ways, we know how they hunt, and we know how to trap and kill them."

"The darkness approaches," Leonidas said. "We must act swiftly."

Within the hour, Leonidas, Falon and two other young village men made their way east toward the caverns at the foothills of the mountain. By late afternoon they had reached the caves where the wolves made their dens. Leonidas surveyed the surrounding area, but saw no evidence of wildfire or flood. A cold wind swept between the rocky crags sending a howling moan through the desolate valley.

Falon struck his flint to light a torch. He stood in the entrance to the largest cave and brandished the flame before him. "I see no signs of a collapse," he said. "The walls appear sound."

The other hunters, Barek and his brother Keurig, lit their own torches and slowly advanced into the cavern past Falon.

Barek lowered his torch to illuminate a half-eaten deer carcass lying in the dirt. "The wolves were here less than a day ago. But why would they leave before finishing their meal?"

Keurig took a few more steps then crouched to inspect the ground. Massive wolf tracks surrounded a trail of boot prints leading further into the cave. Leonidas squinted into the shadows, hearing a low, faint rumble that he thought was the flurry of bats' wings somewhere deep in the cavern. The distant sound grew louder, reverberating throughout the tunnel like the stirrings of an avalanche.

In the darkness beyond Barek and Keurig, two red eyes

suddenly glowed like fierce embers. Before Leonidas could cry out a warning, the ominous rumble resolved itself into a deafening snarl and white, dagger-sharp teeth flashed out of the gloom like a lightning strike and snapped Keurig's arm in two. His torch fell to the cavern floor in a shower of orange sparks. Covered in a spray of the younger man's blood, Leonidas gazed in astonishment at Keurig, who stared back at him in shocked silence. Then Keurig was lifted off his feet by a pair of monstrous black arms and dragged backward into the darkness, screaming. The cavern echoed with Barek's ragged voice, calling his brother's name.

Leonidas and Falon dragged Barek out of the cave into the security of daylight. With his dagger drawn, Barek fought against them, straining to get back into the dark cavern, but Leonidas firmly held him. "Enough!" the older man shouted. "You cannot go back in there. Your brother is dead."

Falon had drawn his bow with trembling hands, waiting for the monster to charge them. "I have never seen a wolf that large," he whispered.

"That was no wolf," Leonidas said, peering into the black depths of the cave. "There may be others in there as well."

"When night falls they will be free to prowl the forests," Falon said. "We cannot allow them to reach the village."

"They are not bound for the village," Leonidas said. "They seek the Tower, and we must stop them before they can get there." The old man's mind raced as he tried to form a plan of attack. Glancing around him, his eyes locked on a sloping meadow in the distance. "Come," he said. "We must work quickly."

As the sun fell below the horizon, Leonidas' dread increased. Alone, he paced back and forth near the copse of trees that acted as a rough gateway to the meadow of blue flowers beyond. Several hundred yards in front of him, the dark maw of the cavern sat silent and still. Glancing overhead, he watched as a veil of clouds drifted across the face of the moon, blotting its light from the night sky. When it reappeared once more, the cold, ethereal moonlight made the black spires of the Tower on the distant mountain appear in stark relief.

His hand, bound in a swatch of cloth torn from his cloak, ached and throbbed, but he forced himself to ignore the pain. A sudden, almost imperceptible flicker of movement in the cavern's entrance caught his attention, and he stopped pacing. Leonidas squinted and saw the familiar twin embers from the afternoon's attack and from his terrible dream. The beast, even larger than the wolf Falon had killed earlier in the day, emerged from the cave, sniffing the ground where Leonidas had begun the trail of blood from his hand. The sight of the monster seemed to make the knife slit in his bound palm pulse even more urgently, and panic began coursing through his body. The creature crept forward on its massive legs, enchanted by the smell of blood, and when it saw Leonidas boldly standing in the open, the beast's eyes widened and it bared its fangs in a garish parody of a smile.

Leonidas held out his hands and gestured for the monster to come forward. "Volkodlak," he called out. "Come meet your damnation."

The beast sprang forward and galloped at top speed toward Leonidas, who leapt aside at the last instant as the creature sailed between two of the trees at the entrance to the meadow. Though his face was pressed down into the grass, Leonidas could hear the mad scrambling of the beast as it tried to stop its forward momentum, and it emitted a defiant, bewildered mewling as its body touched the poisonous blue flowers of the wolfsbane all around it. Leonidas sat up in time to see Falon and Barek in the trees release their arrows at the same time. The arrows sliced into the animal's back, and the creature released a snarling bellow of pain and fury as it writhed in agony amid the toxic blossoms. The monstrous beast frothed at the mouth, and Leonidas watched in disbelief as its dark fur fell off its hide in sickly clumps and its tremendous haunches seemed to shrivel and collapse in on themselves until they took on the form of a man's legs. The immense, fanged snout of the creature receded like melting clay. The visage of the monster withered and settled into the gasping countenance of a dying man.

Barek leapt from his tree, pulling his axe from his pack. Even in the moonlight Leonidas could see that the young man's face was stained with tears of sorrow and rage. He cried out his brother's name as he stood over the fallen wampior, and in one violent stroke he cleaved the fiend's head from his body, ending its abominable existence once and for all.

"Leonidas... behind you," Falon hissed from his perch overhead.

The old man turned to see the silhouettes of two more monstrous wolves lurking at the edge of the meadow. Emerging from the darkness behind the creatures strode a tall man in black robes. As he stepped from the shadows, the moonlight revealed the stranger's features. His eyes were wells of blackness that glistened with rancor and menace. In contrast, his flesh held a deathly pallor that was matched by the ivory hue of his long hair.

Leonidas' blood ran cold as he realized who now stood before them. This was the one of whom the prophecy had warned. This was Dravek, the dreaded white wolf.

Without a word, Dravek stepped into the wolfsbane

patch, and stormed past Leonidas, paying him little heed as he made his way toward the man who had slain his monstrous minion. Barek rushed toward his advancing foe, raising his bloody axe high above him. With a furious cry, Barek leapt into the air and swung the blade down toward Dravek's skull with all his force. Dravek caught the descending axe by the handle and wrenched the weapon from the hunter's hand. Clutching Barek by the throat, Dravek lifted him off his feet, drawing him close to his face. The white-haired ghoul snarled to reveal his fanged mouth, then tore into Barek's throat like a savage beast, gorging himself on the dying man's blood. When all life had left Barek's body, Dravek tossed his corpse to the wolves that stood waiting at the edge of the woods. A frenzy of snapping jaws and gnashing teeth erupted as the beasts tore the carcass to pieces, devouring the dead man's flesh.

Dravek stared off at the distant Tower. "It has been many years since I have visited this region." His low, raspy voice carried the chill of the grave. "I had all but forgotten how savage these lands can be." He turned to Leonidas, wiping the blood from his lips. "Who has sent you here?"

Leonidas stood speechless, desperately searching his own thoughts for an answer that might spare his life, until at last he replied, "The Lord of the Dark Tower."

"Do not try to deceive me." The threat of harsh retribution lurked behind Dravek's words. "I know very well that Lord Brom has abandoned the Tower. Your righteous savior has forsaken you."

"I would not dare lie to you, my lord." Leonidas drew a deep breath, then continued to weave his tale. "It is as you have said, Lord Brom is no longer the master of the Tower... but another has taken his place."

Dravek's black eyes narrowed. "Who?"

"We do not know his name. He is but a shadow in the night, but his magic is strong. He is more powerful than those who came before him. He has foreseen your return and has sent us here to deliver a message."

"Then speak it," Dravek demanded, "while you still have a tongue."

Summoning all his courage, the old man uttered a threatening ultimatum. "Leave these lands at once, or come meet your doom in the Tower."

Dravek's eyes slowly filled with rage but before he could speak a word, a rustling of leaves drew his attention overhead. Scanning the tree where Falon had hidden, his eyes met a solitary raven perched on a low branch.

"The shadow lord sends his emissary," Leonidas whispered.

Dravek kept his eyes locked upon the ebon bird, and the creature stared back at him in silence. A bitter wind rose and swept through the trees, sending the raven fluttering off in the direction of the Tower.

"Only fools rest their faith in empty words," Dravek growled. "There is but one way to know the truth." He turned and stalked past Leonidas toward the waiting wolves. "Come, old one," he said. "You will accompany us to the Tower. We shall see what awaits us there."

Leonidas stood silent and frozen in place as a feeling of dread crept over him.

"Come with us now," Dravek said, "or your flesh shall feed my minions."

Leonidas obeyed the command, following Dravek as he marched into the darkness toward the mountain path. The two monstrous wolves trailed close behind the old man, snarling and bearing their bloodstained fangs. Traveling westward into the night, Leonidas gazed toward the distant mountaintop where tall spires stretched upward like fingers reaching to grasp the rising moon. He had spared his own life for the moment, but he had not deterred Dravek from venturing to the Tower. Tears stung the old man's eyes as he thought of the terrible fate that would befall Vasaria, and perhaps all mankind, once they reached their destination.

Prophecy Foretold

Joseph Iorillo and Joseph Vargo

Amidst a haze of shadows and smoke, a gargantuan dragon, black as night, stirred and wakened from its ancient slumber. The great horned beast rose from the depths of its cavernous lair to emerge high atop a mountain summit. The ferocious creature reared up against the dawning sky and with a thunderous rumble it unfurled its massive wings, blotting out the light of the sun. The beast's diabolic shadow spread across the land like a pool of blood, tainting the world of man beneath its deadly pall. And in the growing darkness, a black sun rose, its crimson halo burning in the sky, heralding the dawn of a sinister new age.

Brom awoke with a start as his carriage traveled over a patch of rough road. Weak moonlight spilled through the coach windows, falling upon the scroll clutched in his hand, illuminating the ancient parchment with a golden glow. As the rocky path rose and wound its way up the mountain, Brom studied the cryptic symbols and impenetrable glyphs decorating the scroll. Though his time amid the volumes and scrolls of the Tower's vast library had given him a formidable command of history and languages long dead, the scroll was written in a tongue that seemed far more ancient than any he had encountered.

Brom glanced out of the window, feeling impatient and restless. He looked for the ominous form of Castle Rankorr upon the mountain but could not discern it yet. A strange new energy coursed through his veins. The Watcher's blood within him invigorated his body and spirit with a newfound strength. The unsettling dream of the black dragon lingered in his thoughts, and Brom took heed of its ominous message, yet he ventured onward fearlessly, fully prepared to face whatever awaited him at the unholy keep.

The rough path became steeper and steeper, and the trees became sparser. The few plants and patches of grass that still clung to the mountainside had a diseased, sickly appearance. The carriage rolled on into a rocky wasteland, and Brom felt a growing unease as the moonlight revealed his savage surroundings of dead trees and jagged boulders blackened and scorched by vicious lightning strikes. The carriage jolted to a sudden stop as the horses reared up on their hind legs and snorted in panic. Brom climbed out of the coach and gazed upon Castle Rankorr. The sprawling fortress loomed in the mist-shrouded night like a sinister cathedral built to honor the lords of darkness. Massive, monolithic stone walls, roughly hewn from dark granite, soared upward to impossible heights and were lost in wisps of clouds far above. Twisting spires reached upward like skeletal fingers, and an army of grim stone beasts peered down upon him from shadowed alcoves along castle ledges. As clouds drifted across the face of the full moon, the sinister gargoyles seemed to stir from the roosts.

Brom's heart filled with unease as he gazed upon the monstrous, hellish revelry captured in gleaming stone. Winged serpents entwined rows of tall pillars, their tails coiled around human skulls. Beastly men with fangs gnawed upon the bones of their victims and devilish fiends with twisted horns leered from the shadows. High above this spectacle, more stone demons clung to the castle's battlements, watching and waiting in silence.

A colossal iron portcullis sealed the castle's arched entryway. As Brom approached it, he heard a distant rumbling that seemed to emanate from the mountain itself. The thunderous sound was punctuated by the metallic squeal of gears grinding against heavy chains. The portcullis rose slowly, like the fanged jaws of some enormous beast, and Brom stood staring into the absolute blackness of the castle's gaping maw.

After a moment, a cloaked figure emerged from the darkness.

"I have awaited your arrival," the figure said. "Come forth, brother."

Brom's warrior instincts had exerted themselves and he glanced around him, noting the terrain and any lurking threats. Finally he stepped through the castle gate into the foreboding domain of the Black Dawn.

The smell of decay, which had been subtle outside of the gate, became more powerful, as if Brom were entering a mass grave. The cloaked figure spoke again, quieter than before. "I am Brother Grigori. Welcome to Castle Rankorr, Lord Brom."

"How do you know my name?"

"I know many secrets, my lord."

Brom cast a scrutinizing gaze upon the old man. "You are a sorcerer."

"I am a seer. I possess the gift of sight beyond all obstacles, even time."

"Does the future hold no secrets from you?"

"Very few," the old man said. "Most men follow their fated paths without deviation, yet there are some who stray from their destined course."

The seer escorted Brom through the castle's inner courtyard, where several guards clad in heavy black armor stood on either side of the keep's entrance, watching them at a distance, their scarred, muscular hands resting on the hilts of their sheathed broadswords. Jagged shafts of ethereal blue moonlight fell across some of the guards, making them resemble ghastly statues of hell-born demons. Fierce eyes glistened behind blackened steel helmets fashioned in the likeness of wolfish skulls. Brom was careful to keep his face concealed within the shadows of his hood.

The heavy iron doors of the castle stood ajar, revealing the meager glow of torches mounted along the inner corridor walls. Once inside, Brom's uneasiness grew perceptibly as he noticed the ornate carvings of dragons, griffons and loathsome serpents on the walls. The flickering firelight created the illusion of movement, making it seem as if the sculpted beasts were writhing and spreading their wings.

"Where are you taking me?" Brom asked.

"To someplace more discreet. We must speak in privacy. No one here knows who you truly are, my lord. You must rest your trust in me."

Brom followed Grigori silently up a narrow staircase and down a darkened hall to a massive oaken door. The seer opened the door to reveal a surprisingly lush, inviting chamber adorned with colorful tapestries, velvet drapes, silken curtains and numerous silver candelabras. At the far end of the chamber, a lovely young woman with dark hair stood pensively on the stone balcony, framed by the window arch and illuminated by the moon's cold bluish light. Her eyes were full of dread and fear, but when she saw Brom the fear seemed to diminish palpably. Brom gazed at her for a long moment, taken with her almond-shaped eyes and her expression of solemn innocence and apprehension. There were echoes of Rianna in this girl, but perhaps this was merely the magic of longing and nostalgia.

"Lord Brom," the seer said, "allow me to introduce my cherished daughter, Serena."

"My father has spoken of you often," Serena said in a quiet voice. "His visions have foretold of your coming. But now, as you stand here before me, I realize you have entered my own dreams as well."

Brom stood silent, intrigued by the girl's whispered words.

Serena spoke again. "I have had the vision many times whilst I slept, and each time it is the same. It begins with a woman in white, a radiant angel with a wounded wing. She stands upon a mountain ledge, trapped between the heavens above and the earth far below. She teeters on the edge of the precipice, longing to fly free once more, but alas, she is bound to her earthly domain. As she stands balanced on the brink of despair, a shadow falls across the sun, transforming the day to blackest night.

In the encompassing gloom, a dark angel, handsome and lean, descends upon leathery wings. Seeing the forlorn beauty stranded on the rocky ledge, he hastens to her side, pulling her close and sweeping her up into his strong arms. Spreading his ebon wings, he carries her aloft, taking to flight across the darkened sky. The two soar ever higher together until at last he returns her to the heavens where she rests safe from harm." The girl's lips formed a slight smile as she ended her tale. "As I have said, I have dreamt it many times, and the vision is clear in my mind. The dark angel of my dream... it is you, Lord Brom."

Serena searched Brom's eyes for a hint of emotion, but

found none there. "Have you come to help us?" she asked. Brom glanced at the seer. "My purpose here is... unclear."

The look of despair returned to the girl's eyes and she said nothing more as she retreated back into the room.

Grigori turned and led Brom down the hall to a shadowed alcove that concealed a secret door. The old man slid a key into a hidden lock and twisted it. The heavy door creaked open to reveal a narrow, winding stairwell leading down. Their footfalls echoed hollowly in the nighttime stillness, and the air grew colder as they descended. The stairs ended in a chamber cluttered with charts and diagrams inscribed on tattered parchment, animal and human skulls, and ancient stone ritual figurines from bygone eras. Hanging on the far wall was a large tapestry depicting a knight driving a long blade into the heart of a black winged dragon, the two beings locked in mortal combat amidst a swirl of fire and smoke. At the center of the room, twin dragons of wrought iron supported a shallow copper cauldron of burning coals.

The seer's eyes grew bright in the fiery glow. "You seek the truth hidden in the scroll that you carry. I can decipher its meaning, but I seek something in return."

Brom stared at him coldly. "I will not aid the Black Dawn's rise."

The old man shook his head. "I am no disciple of their blasphemous beliefs. The favor I seek is not for their benefit, or even my own. It is for my daughter, Serena. I wish to spare her a lifetime of darkness so that she may live free of misery and fear."

"Then take her from this place," Brom said.

Grigori's voice grew weak. "I would, if it were only possible."

"I see no chains binding her here. Or you."

"None that are visible," the seer said. He attempted a feeble smile. "But there is much that lurks beneath the surface here. Allow me to tell you my tale." The old man turned away and gazed into the cauldron of burning coals. "My daughter and I lived in the village in the shadow of this keep. That village is little more than a scorched patch of earth and ash now. Even I, in my discerning wisdom, did not foresee the storm until it was upon us.

The seer turned his eyes back to Brom. "You know of Dravek, do you not?"

Brom recalled the vile name from tales of the Tower's history.

"He was once a servant of the Dark Queen—a creature of the night, tainted with Mara's blood. He was slain by the Baron during his siege of the Dark Tower."

Grigori stepped closer, lowering his voice to a grave whisper. "He is a devil born of Mara's unholy blood, this is true, but he did not die at the hands of the Baron. He survived to plot his vengeful wrath."

The seer circled the fiery cauldron, pacing slowly around the glowing hearth. "The lords who once ruled here thought Castle Rankorr to be invulnerable to conquest. Throughout the generations the keep withstood countless enemy assaults and sieges without being toppled or breached. Yet, one man alone did what entire armies could not.

"Dravek came to the castle like a wolf in the night, murdering the guards, then slaying the king. His strength and speed were unmatched by the mortal warriors he faced. The halls ran red with the blood he spilled. He released the prisoners in the dungeon, but bound them in a dark pact. Those who swore allegiance to him became his soldiers—the first legion of the Black Dawn. The rest met with a terrible fate."

"Once the castle was his, Dravek unleashed his horde upon the village. All who resisted felt his cruel wrath. Those who did not join him were put to death. Entire families were slaughtered."

"Yet, you and your daughter are very much alive," Brom said.

"My life was spared because my powers were useful to Dravek's plan. But he was cunning enough to realize that threats of death or violence toward me would not make me his slave. Seeing that I cherished my daughter's life more than my own, Dravek's threats fell upon her. I am forced to do his bidding only because Serena's life hangs in the balance. Though she is allowed the freedom of the castle and its grounds, she cannot leave. As long as she remains here, I am in his thrall. I can help you, Lord Brom, but only if you vow to release her from this bondage."

Brom stood by the seer's cauldron, looking into the reddish orange eyes of the smoldering coals. He thought of the girl, held against her will within the castle's bleak, oppressive walls, and he considered the seer's tale. Brom was in the domain of an enemy nearly as treacherous as the blasphemous horror entombed beneath the Dark Tower, and many years of bitter experience told him that deception and lies were often the weapons of evil. He did not know if the old man and his beautiful daughter were indeed captives here or merely pawns in Dravek's dark scheme.

After a long moment, Brom spoke. "I will do all I can for your daughter."

The seer stared deep into Brom's eyes, as if peering into his soul, then nodded, betraying no emotion. "You must be wary, my lord. Dravek is sly. He has bided his time, amassing his forces, waiting for the appropriate time to strike. Through the years, he has gathered a legion of loyal minions who have dedicated their lives to serving him in his quest to resurrect the Dark Queen."

"Why has Dravek not returned to Vasaria in all these years?"

The seer turned away and stood silent for a long moment. At last he said, "He fears you, my lord. Only by a twist of fate did he escape his doom at the hands of the Baron. He dared not challenge him again. When the Baron passed his legacy to you, Dravek devised a plan. He has many followers who obey his commands without question. They call themselves the Brotherhood of the Black Dawn.

"Years ago, Dravek sent one such minion to Vasaria to test your strength and resolve. Torin was his name. He foolishly sought to avenge his dead father by killing the Baron. Instead, he met his own demise, slain by your hand, Lord Brom."

Brom dimly recalled the trespasser who came to the Tower many years ago. "Why would Dravek send him to meet certain doom?"

The seer looked at him. "Because Torin's true mission was to deliver a vital artifact—the key to the catacombs below the Tower, so that you might unlock the path to Mara's tomb. Dravek believed that you would not be able to resist the Dark Queen's enchantments once you had ventured within her unholy grasp."

Though Brom could feel the heat from the burning coals, an icy chill crept through him as he remembered his sojourn in the catacombs, a grim journey that had brought him to a brief spiritual communion with Mara's lethal essence. He recalled her captivating beauty, her lustrous raven-black hair and the indescribable, hypnotic thrill he felt when her warm lips touched his and her slender fingers danced over his skin....

It had been but a transient vision, yet the awe-inspiring power of the Dark Queen had left its mark on the core of his being.

"I am forced to do Dravek's bidding," the seer said. "I tell him of my visions, but I have not revealed all to him. I foresaw your coming here and I know of the scroll you carry, but I have kept many things secret. My reasons are not as noble as yours. I have concealed the truth from Dravek for my daughter's sake. Her salvation rests in your hands."

"As my fate rests in yours." Brom replied, unrolling the scroll for the seer's inspection. "I must learn its message and you are my only key to this."

The old man's eyes studied the parchment briefly before moving to the tapestry on the wall. He pulled the woven portrait aside, revealing an inscription etched deeply into the castle's worn stones. Brom recognized the runic symbols as the glyphs on the scroll.

"This inscription is older than recorded history," the seer said. "The ancient scribes deciphered its meaning and passed its cryptic message down through the generations. I am the last to know of it. The inscription relates the tale of the scribe Enoch, who chronicled the Dark Ones' fall from Heaven and their subsequent exile on Earth. They came to beget children with mortals, but they were no heavenly creatures. Their offspring inherited their unearthly powers, with grievous results."

Grigori held out his hand, saying "If you will permit me, my lord."

With some hesitation, Brom placed the scroll in the seer's hand. The old man's eyes washed over the ancient symbols as he studied them intently. "The message of the scroll is older than the tale of Enoch," Grigori said. "Some of the words are beyond my understanding. I shall need more time for a precise translation, but I can tell you all I know."

In a low, clear voice, the old man intoned:
"In the time of great darkness,
the immortal one shall rise...
destroyer and bringer of death...
The secrets of the trinity shall be revealed,
and the chalice of eternal life shall be found...
One shall decide the fate of all men...
By supreme decree,
the Seraphim shall hold dominion over the Earth."

"Seraphim," Brom said, a trace of wonder in his voice. "Do you mean angels?"

"Or possibly the Fallen Ones," the seer replied. "I will need to study it further to decipher its full meaning." The old man went to a rough table laden with tools and parchments. He ran his finger along the hilt of a silver dagger, and a grim expression overtook his weathered features. "I sense you will need this." He offered Brom the gleaming blade.

"A mere dagger to vanquish one as powerful as Dravek?"

"Not Dravek. Ramiel. He is Dravek's warlord, commanding his master's shadow warriors. He is as you are, Lord Brom—a creature of the night. The blood of the Fallen Ones courses through his veins. While his followers and castle guards are merely the lowest of men, his legions in the dungeons below the keep are mindless thralls, abominations born of the blackest sorcery. Their soulless bodies are simply husks of the men they once were. They have been reduced to bloodthirsty beasts with inhuman appetites.

"The Black Dawn is a slumbering dragon. Before it wakes, it can be felled with one strike. To slay this serpent, all you need do is sever its head. Vanquish Ramiel and his army will be lost, scattering to the shadows to wither and die."

Brom reluctantly accepted the dagger and slid it into his belt under his cloak. "Creatures of darkness possess heightened senses, like wolves. If Ramiel draws near, he will detect that I am no mortal man."

The seer lit a shaft of incense and walked slowly around Brom. A fragrant blue smoke enveloped Brom in a ghostly cloud that quickly dissipated. "This will mask your scent from Ramiel. When you are taken to meet him, do not try to deceive him, for he will know if your words are lies. Choose your words carefully and he will remain blinded to the truth."

A moment later the thunder of footfalls could be heard descending the stone stairwell. Two of the armed guards from the courtyard stood in the entryway. "Brother Ramiel has returned from his hunt and awaits his guest," one of the guards said in a gruff, brutish voice.

The seer nodded and turned to Brom, looking him steadily in the eye. "Go with them," he said quietly. "I will join you once I have completed my work."

Brom followed the guards out of the chamber. As the sound of footsteps receded, the seer returned to the burning cauldron and gazed deeply into the fiery coals. He then turned once again to study the inscription graven upon the stone wall. Stepping to a writing table, he placed the scroll beside a stack of blank sheets and bowed his head with a solemn cast. His hand trembled as he set quill to parchment and grimly began his chronicle of all he had seen.

In the fullness of time, a new sun shall rise over the Earth, a black dawn that shall allow those born of the night to live freely in this world and rule as befits our power and our nature. My darkness shall reign over all, and no light shall prevail against it.

—Mara, The Dark Queen

The Beast Within

JOSEPH VARGO

The sound of heavy footfalls echoed through the dim stone corridor as four armored guards marched Brom deep into the black heart of Castle Rankorr. Torches blazed in iron sconces set at intervals along the walls, creating pockets of auburn light between long stretches of darkness. Each time he approached an area of torchlight, Brom lowered his hooded head, keeping his face hidden from the soldiers that surrounded him. His mission thus far had been one of stealth and secrecy, yet if his escorts so much as suspected his true identity, Brom knew he would have to take action against them.

The men ascended a broad stone staircase that wound its way high above an empty banquet hall blanketed by layers of cobwebs and dust. Reaching the top of the stairway, Brom and his escorts marched along a lengthy corridor adorned with suits of ancient armor and tapestries depicting fierce legendary beasts. After several turns, they proceeded toward an arched doorway flanked by two more guards. The twin doors beneath the arch displayed a pair of rampant wolves etched deep into the knotted wood.

The castle guards herded Brom into the darkened room then turned and left without a word, closing the heavy doors behind them. Columns of black stone supported archways along the perimeter of the chamber, but the windows within the alcoves had been sealed with bricks and mortar, keeping the room sequestered in shadows. The chiseled faces of leering demons adorned the columns lining the chamber walls. The diabolic sculptures held burning torches in their open mouths, illuminating the dim room with a hellish glow.

At the far end of the chamber, twin dragons of stone stood guard at the sides of a flaming hearth. A tall figure, no more than a black silhouette, waited before the fire. The shadow faced away from Brom as it gazed into the writhing flames.

A low, coarse voice echoed across the room. "Brother Grigori has foreseen your arrival. He has told me of your plight in the monastery."

Brom kept his eyes locked upon the mysterious figure but said nothing.

The shadow spoke again. "He has told me that the dark lord of Vasaria has ventured to your sacred temple and that you now seek safe haven among our ranks."

The figure turned and stepped forward into a halo of torchlight. He met Brom's eyes with a piercing gaze. His black hair and trimmed beard were accented by streaks of silver. His broad shoulders bore the raiments of a regal warlord. A tunic and cape of deep crimson draped armor of blackened leather. A dark insignia emblazoned upon the front of his blood-red vestment depicted an ebon circle surrounded by a halo of twisting spikes. Brom recognized the design as the emblem of the Black Dawn.

"Rest your worries, brother," the dark knight said, his deep voice hypnotic and soothing, "for as long as you remain among our fold, you shall have nothing to fear. I am Ramiel, commander of the Black Dawn. I offer you the sanctuary of our fortress."

"Are you, then, the lord of this castle?" Brom asked.

Ramiel's eyes narrowed. "No. My master, Lord Dravek, is away. I am his voice in his absence." As the warlord stepped closer, his shadow stretched across a heavy wooden table in the center of the chamber.

Brom remained where he stood, keeping a cautious distance from the advancing knight. "You have said that Brother Grigori foretold of my mission here. How could he have known this?"

"He is gifted with sight beyond mortal vision," Ramiel said. "Nothing escapes his mystic gaze. Through him, we see and know all." The warlord slowed to a halt. "He has also foretold of a scroll—a manuscript of ancient wisdom, sought by the dark lord."

Brom's mind raced as he recalled the words of the seer. The old man had warned him not to lie, but to choose his words carefully. "Yes," Brom said. "It is a treasured artifact from the reliquary vaults of the priory. It is said to hold a great prophecy concerning the Tower Lord, but the words scribed upon it are beyond my comprehension."

"Where is it now?" Ramiel asked.

"I have delivered it to Brother Grigori, so that he may decipher its divine message."

A slight smile formed on Ramiel's lips. He moved closer and beckoned to Brom, saying, "Come forth, brother."

Brom slowly advanced toward him, wary of each step he took. The two men met at opposite sides of the central table. Ramiel's face and hands were drained of all color and Brom detected the scent of death upon him. The warlord stood silent, staring at Brom like a wolf sizing its prey. At last, he directed Brom's attention to the table between them. A broadsword rested within Ramiel's reach, its battle-worn blade spattered with blood. Beneath the sword, a large map of the region lay sprawled across the worm-eaten planks.

"Your priory lies well within the dark lord's grasp." Ramiel swept his hand across the map, allowing its shadow to linger upon the location of the monastery. "For as long as we have known, the Tower Lord has remained sealed within his keep, but he now ventures outward to ravage the land, invading the sanctity of your hallowed halls, no doubt seeking victims to quench his unholy desires. If his venom spreads, all in its path will surely wither and die."

Brom took notice of the locations of Castle Rankorr and the Monastery of St. Sebastian in relation to the Dark Tower. The three castles were equal distances from one another, forming a perfect triangle over the region.

Ramiel rested his hand beside the sword on the table. "We have waited many years, silently mounting our forces to vanquish this blight before it spreads."

Brom contemplated the warlord's plan. "In all this time, why have you not seized the Tower to wrest control from its dark master?"

"Only a fool would attack a serpent while it lies coiled in its lair," Ramiel hissed. "A lifetime of war and battle has taught me much. Long ago, I knew nothing of strategy. Blind action was my only course." Ramiel's fingers ran along the jagged edge of the sword's blade. "Reckless youth empowers men with a boldness and strength to defy the elements and venture headstrong into uncharted lands. But there is much risk in such action. I have since come to know that a solid strategy is the backbone of victory.

"With age comes the wisdom to allow the winds to dictate your course." Ramiel's gaze fell upon the map once more. "The winds of change are now upon us. At long last, the dark lord has ventured forth from the Tower, leaving the keep vulnerable to siege."

An icy chill grasped Brom's heart as he realized the dire gravity of his situation. His enemies plotted to strike the Tower in his absence, unaware that he now stood in their midst. Brom's only thought was to engage Ramiel further to learn more of his plan.

"Do you think it wise to breech the unholy keep?" Brom asked. "It is said that the Dark Tower rests upon the tomb of an evil spirit—the wicked queen of a sinister brood, born of the blood of fallen angels. Legends say that her body lies entombed in the catacombs beneath the keep and that her dark soul is cursed to dwell within the confines of the Tower for all eternity."

Ramiel scoffed at Brom's words. "Do not be swayed by the tales of superstitious minds. They fear all that is unknown, imagining evil beneath every shadow."

Brom met the warlord's gaze with a solemn stare. "It is said that evil dwells in the hearts of all men."

"Perhaps that is true," Ramiel said. "Most men are foolish and weak. Their fears lead them to create false masters and serve them as slaves. Throughout the ages they have worshipped countless idols. Rivers have run red with the blood they have spilled in the name of their gods, yet their prayers go unanswered." Ramiel lifted the sword from the table. "My faith lies in the power of my will and the strength of my steel. The blood I spill slakes only my own thirst." As he spoke, firelight gleamed in his eyes. "The decayed remnants of the old world must be toppled and destroyed before a better world can be forged."

Brom stood silent and still, weighing the warlord's words carefully, until at last he spoke. "I too, was once a man of war. Though it was many years ago, I recall my past life all too clearly." Brom stared at the map before him. "I followed my faith to commit grievous acts, witnessing terrible deeds that haunt me still. I survived the horrors of battle to face an unimaginable foe. I escaped my death once more, but only at great cost. I succumbed to a fate far more desolate than the grave itself. Since that day, I have dedicated my existence to vanquishing evil in all its earthly forms. Again and again, destiny's call has led me into darkness, as it led me here this night. And each time I ventured into the abyss, I have emerged stronger than before."

Ramiel stared across the table, studying Brom with a piercing gaze, as if trying to penetrate his innermost thoughts. Brom felt Ramiel's mind probing his own, but Brom's powers were far greater, allowing him to shield his memories and thoughts from the warlord's magic. The two men sat locked in a silent war of wills until a knock at the chamber door broke the spell.

"Enter," Ramiel bellowed.

Grigori entered the room, closing the heavy door behind him. "I have translated the scroll from the monastery, my lord." The seer's voice held a submissive, almost fearful tremor.

"Bring it forth," Ramiel commanded.

The old man hastened to the warlord's side like a faithful hound, carrying two scrolls, one ancient and one new.

"This is the scroll from the priory vaults," Grigori said quietly, offering Ramiel the tattered document Brom had delivered.

The warlord unrolled the weathered scroll and laid it on the table before him. His eyes washed over its strange, unrecognizable symbols with little interest.

"And this is the translated prophecy," the seer said,

handing Ramiel the unblemished scroll.

The warlord unrolled the crisp parchment, but held it close, allowing no one else to see it. Brom glanced at the seer to assess his loyalty. He recognized a hint of unease in the old man's eyes, but sensed no signs of betrayal.

Ramiel's gaze remained fixed on the scroll as he studied its message intently.

"What does it say?" Brom asked.

Ramiel glared at him. "You need not concern yourself with its contents," the warlord said tersely. "All you need know is that it foretells the rise of the Dark Queen, and assures our victory in the battle we wage."

Brom's eyes shifted to Grigori. The old man stepped slowly to the hearth at the far end of the chamber, as if summoned and entranced by the fire within.

"What do you see?" Ramiel asked.

The seer gazed deep into the serpentine flames. "I see black walls, stained red with blood. A towering keep lies engulfed in flames beneath the full moon's light. The beast that rages within shall be unleashed, and all who dare to stand against it shall fall." The seer's eyes remained transfixed upon the fire, but he said no more.

Ramiel smiled, revealing long, wolfish fangs, then thrust his sword down into the table, driving it deep into the rough wood. "We have long waited in shadows and silence," he growled. "Our time of reckoning has come."

"How so?" Brom asked. "Your queen lies dead, vanquished and entombed beneath the Tower of Vasaria. Her crypt is protected—guarded by those sworn to destroy you."

"The Dark Queen lies imprisoned, that is true, but she cannot be slain. She is the earthly vessel of Lilith, mother of all who dwell in the night. She merely slumbers in her tomb, awaiting her follower's return. Once she is freed, she shall unleash a wrath beyond all reckoning. The Black Dawn shall rise, plummeting the earth into night without end, and in the darkness, we shall reign supreme."

"And what of freedom?" Brom asked. "Shall all men serve as slaves to your grim empire?"

"Those who do not worship the Dark Queen shall be trampled beneath her armies." Ramiel's voice grew louder in anger. "The weak shall serve the strong, or die like slaughtered beasts."

Brom's dark eyes filled with rage. "You would unleash this demon to bestow torment and death upon all who do not worship her? Once this plague is released, it shall destroy everything in its path. Your plan is madness."

"Enough!" Ramiel barked, pounding his fist into the table with enough force to splinter the wood. "My patience is at an end. Your insolence has sealed your fate!"

Furious beyond reason, the warlord threw the table aside and lunged toward Brom to deliver a stabbing thrust with his sword. Brom reacted with inhuman speed, catching Ramiel's arm and wrenching it downward with incredible force, shattering the sword's blade against the floor. Brom's iron grip tightened around Ramiel's wrist, snapping the warlord's bones like brittle twigs. Brom's other hand clutched Ramiel's throat, digging his sharp nails deep into the warlord's neck, holding him helplessly captive. Ramiel struggled in vain against Brom's choking grasp.

Brom drew Ramiel's face close to his. "My fate was sealed long ago," Brom whispered, "when I ventured to the Tower of Vasaria. I have known naught but darkness and torment in my years with this curse. I have lost all that I once cherished. I have known suffering far beyond the pain of death, all because of your vile queen. She holds no salvation for mankind, she is the harbinger of misery, death and destruction. And I shall not rest until I have vanquished her soul for all time."

The rage in Ramiel's eyes faded to a look of bewilderment and terror. "How can this be?" he gasped.

"Your seer has deceived you," Brom said, "and in your blind arrogance, you have welcomed your own enemy into your fold."

"Guards!" Ramiel's shout fell hoarse as Brom's nails tore deeper into his throat.

The chamber doors burst open and six armored men swarmed into the room to surround Brom. Each held a broadsword, drawn and at the ready.

Brom lifted Ramiel off his feet and threw him into the guards. The warlord smashed against his soldiers, toppling two men before crashing into the chamber wall. Before the guards could regroup, Brom lashed out with the ferocity of a savage lion. His claws sliced through the air like daggers, tearing open the throats of two attacking warriors. Their lifeless bodies dropped to the floor in a rain of their own blood. Another guard lunged at Brom from behind, swinging his sword down toward Brom's head, but the Tower Lord moved too swiftly. Brom whirled and caught the descending sword, snapping it in two, then plunged the broken blade deep into his attacker's eye, brutally ending his life. As another guard thrust his blade toward Brom's heart, his arm met with Brom's deadly talons. The attacker's hand still clutched its sword as it flew from the man's wrist in a spray of crimson. Before the wounded warrior could utter a scream of pain, Brom tore the man's throat from his neck.

The last two attackers circled Brom slowly, keeping their distance from the mysterious cloaked figure who had effortlessly dispatched their comrades, searching for some weakness to exploit. One guard attempted to deliver a stabbing strike to Brom's exposed back, but the Tower Lord's keen senses alerted him to the man's attack. With lightning speed, Brom plucked the sword from his assailant's hand and thrust it back at him, driving the blade through the warrior's steel breastplate and deep into his chest, stilling the man's heart.

The final soldier raised his sword and lunged forth with a fierce, frenzied cry. Brom swiftly dodged the attack and caught the guard's head, snapping his neck with a violent twist, silencing him instantly.

Brom stood unscathed amidst the carnage he had wrought. His eyes darted around the dim chamber as he quickly surveyed his surroundings. Six men lay dead at his feet, but Ramiel was nowhere to be seen. Brom glanced at the overturned table in the center of the room. The warlord's map lay on the floor beneath it, but the scroll and its translation were gone.

At the far end of the chamber, Brom found Grigori collapsed beside the fireplace. The old man sat slumped against one of the stone dragons that guarded the hearth. The hilt of Ramiel's broken sword protruded from the seer's chest. The dying man stared into the fire where the final vestiges of the two scrolls burned to ash and cinders.

"The scroll is lost," Grigori said, "but its prophecy is not. My daughter knows its secrets. Honor your promise... take her from this place. Once she is safe, she will reveal all she knows."

Grigori's blood-drenched hands clutched the hilt of the blade in his chest. "The dawn has broken," he said. "Ramiel cannot leave the castle. He has fled to the darkness below."

Brom's eyes followed the seer's gaze to an open

passageway in the stone wall beside the hearth.

"He is wounded," Grigori whispered, "but you cannot allow him to survive." The seer clutched Brom's sleeve. "Beware," the old man whispered, "the dungeons hold Dravek's undead legions—monstrous creatures of shadow and darkness. Let none escape." The old man's hand slipped from Brom's arm. "Go. Quickly."

Brom entered the secret passage and followed a narrow, twisting staircase as it burrowed its way deep into the castle bedrock. He emerged in a dungeon corridor near an intersection where four hallways met. Torches hung in sconces along several low, vaulted passageways that led away in different directions. The foul stench of mildew and decay hung thick in the air and distant wails echoed through the foreboding corridors. Brom's eyes scanned the surrounding halls. Droplets of blood stained the stone floor, betraying the wounded warlord's path. Brom followed the trail of crimson down a narrow corridor, past locked gates and bolted doors. In the distance ahead, Brom spied Ramiel, crouching over a fallen guard who lay sprawled on the floor. Brom hastened his pace and the warlord vanished around a corner. As Brom drew nearer, he discovered a grisly scene. The guard lay dead, his throat torn open, his body drained of blood.

Brom quickly resumed the warlord's trail, like a wolf stalking its prey. Turning a corner, he saw Ramiel, staggering along the corridor ahead. Brom pursued him through a roughly chiseled archway into an immense, dimly lit chamber. Ramiel desperately hobbled past a long row of gated prison cells until he reached an alcove at the far end of the room.

Wounded and trapped, the warlord turned to face his relentless pursuer. Brom advanced warily past the empty cells, his eyes darting quickly over his surroundings. A single torch offered the chamber's only illumination, yet large casks of oily pitch were stockpiled in the corner of the room. A massive portcullis sealed a tall archway in the middle of one wall and the crumbling rim of a well spanned the center of the chamber. A mesh of thick iron bars formed a grate that covered the top of the pit.

Ramiel's trembling hand grasped a wooden lever in the wall and thrust it downward. A heavy iron gate slammed shut behind Brom, sealing the dungeon cellblock. The warlord threw another lever and a second gate crashed down between the two men, enclosing Ramiel in the alcove, safely separating him from Brom.

A rasping laugh rose from Ramiel's torn throat. "You have strayed from your sacred vigil, Lord Brom, leaving your post unguarded. My master has ventured to the Dark Tower and he shall soon hold dominion there."

Brom offered no response. He continued to step toward the caged warlord, cautiously circumventing the rim of the foreboding well. Rats scurried past his feet, scampering amidst piles of human bones.

"Long ago," Ramiel growled, "I led the barbarian hordes against the Balkan forces that held this keep. It was a glorious battle beneath thunderous skies. As the tempest raged overhead, my warriors fought with the fury of frenzied demons. But as we stood on the verge of conquest, we were swarmed by the Balkan legions. I was captured and imprisoned here. I thought I would surely meet my end in this vile, forsaken place... but fate had yet to run its course.

"In Dravek's siege of the castle, he found me in chains, caged in my cell like a savage beast. Though I was within Death's grasp, he saw in me a familiar fire, matching the flame that burned in his own heart. He shared his immortality with me, rescuing me from a lingering demise in this place. For that, I swore my allegiance to him. Many of the other prisoners vowed to serve him as well. The ones who did not were cast into the pit, where they yet dwell in the black depths." Ramiel gestured to the well in the center of the chamber. "They are the undying legions of the Black Dawn."

Brom peered down into the pit beside him. The rancid stench of decay issued forth from the abysmal depths. There, far beneath the iron grate, shambling forms stirred in the shadows. The loathsome abominations that lurked below were no longer mortal men. Rotting flesh clung to their bones and their vacant, unblinking eyes stared blankly into the lightless void. Their skeletal arms reached upward as they shrieked for release.

The warlord's lips twisted to form a sinister smile. "Dravek's blood empowered them with immortality and his magic transformed them into creatures of darkness, obedient to his every command, but there was one that grew beyond my master's control, becoming a ravenous beast, more monstrous and fierce than any fiend from Hell. We dared not set it loose upon the night for fear of the havoc it would wreak."

Ramiel turned a large crank wheel that resembled the winch of a drawbridge and the sound of heavy chains grating against stone echoed throughout the room. Brom turned to see the gate at his side slowly lift, opening the passage in the wall of the chamber.

A deep growling sound emanated from the dark recesses of the cavernous cell. Skeletal remains littered the floor and streaks of dried blood stained the walls. Brom's muscles tensed in anticipation as a hulking form crept forth from the shadows, crunching skulls and bones beneath its every step. If the creature had once been a man, it retained few vestiges of

humanity. The thing lumbering in the darkness resembled an enormous, hairless bat. The monstrous beast stood upright, towering over Brom as it sniffed the stale air. Its leathery flesh held a ghoulish pallor, whiter than ash. Its eyes were orbs of black, sunk deep into their sockets, and pointed ears rose from its hideous head.

The hellish beast locked its black eyes on Brom and snarled to reveal fangs long as daggers. Its drooling mouth gaped wide and it emitted a ferocious shriek. The creature spread its arms, unfolding massive wings that spanned the entire archway.

Ever so slowly, Brom took a step backward, inching away from the living nightmare before him, but before he could take a second step, the monstrous bat sprang forth from its cave. Brom dropped low, narrowly dodging the attack and the creature sailed past, tearing Brom's cloak with its talons.

Before the creature turned to face him again, Brom bounded across the room, seeking the torch beside the entrance gate, but the monster moved with lightning speed to thwart Brom's plan. Before Brom could reach the torch the creature was upon him. Brom leapt aside, narrowly escaping the beast's gnashing teeth and monstrous talons. The demon crashed into the portcullis, bending the bars of the gate. Brom retreated toward the center of the room, leaning back against the well's stone rim.

The hellish bat sniffed the spatters of Ramiel's blood on the floor and its cold, black eyes scanned the room. The creature issued a bloodcurdling screech, then leapt into the air, clutching the stones of the wall, climbing to the shadowed heights of the vaulted ceiling.

Brom remained motionless. His eyes searched the chamber for weapons, but there were none to be found.

Remembering the dagger the seer had given him, Brom slowly reached for his belt. But as Brom shifted his weight, a small stone fell from the crumbling lip of the well into the pit below. The scant sound betrayed Brom's location. The winged beast swooped from the shadows above, crashing down on top of Brom, holding him captive beneath its crushing weight.

The creature's talons dug deep into Brom's shoulders, pinning him to the grate that covered the pit. Brom clutched the monster's throat with one hand, holding its snapping jaws at bay while his other hand groped for the silver dagger in his belt. Taking hold of the weapon, Brom thrust the blessed silver blade into the beast's throat, searing its flesh and severing the tendons of its jaw. The demonic creature shrieked and writhed in agony. As it flailed its neck, the dagger fell loose, dropping into the well below. A cacophony of wails and savage growls erupted from the undead legions of the pit.

Blood seeped from the wounds in Brom's shoulders, and he could feel his vitality waning with each new pulse. The creature's mouth drew ever closer to Brom's throat. With his last ounce of strength, Brom dug his clawed hand into the monster's abdomen, thrusting it upward, beneath the beast's ribcage, gripping its black heart and tearing it from the demon's chest. The monstrous beast convulsed in violent spasms, then fell silent and still. Brom pushed the ungodly creature aside and stood to face Ramiel. The great bat lay dead. Dark blood pooled on the flagstones beneath the monster and spread across the floor.

A look of astonishment washed over the warlord's face. "You are a mighty warrior indeed, Lord Brom, powerful and fierce," Ramiel uttered in a raspy whisper, "but your battle is lost. Dravek has gone to the Tower and nothing shall stand in his way."

Brom stepped toward the gated alcove, but stopped beside one of the casks of oil. A swipe of his bloodied hand toppled the heavy barrel, spilling its contents onto the floor. The black oil crept across the flagstones toward Ramiel.

The warlord's eyes widened in panic as he watched the oil seep beneath the gate, covering the floor beneath him. "Mara shall rise to rule the land once more," he screamed. "The Black Dawn shall cover the earth in darkness. You cannot defeat us... we are immortal!"

"No, Ramiel," Brom said, "your humanity was lost long ago, 'tis true." Brom took the chamber torch from its sconce. "But you are not immortal." Brom lowered the torch to the ground, igniting the oily spill. Flames rushed across the floor to fill the gated alcove with blazing fire. Within seconds, Ramiel was engulfed in a blinding inferno. His howling screams echoed throughout the dungeon as the ravaging flames consumed him.

Brom took hold of a second cask of the black pitch. He hoisted the massive barrel over his head and heaved it onto the grate that sealed the pit. It crashed against the bars and burst to pieces. The oil poured through the gate, drenching the vile creatures in the cavern below. The wailing screams of the imprisoned legion rose to a screeching pitch. Brom dropped his torch into the well, setting fire to the pit, sending the monstrous creatures within to their long-awaited deaths.

Retracing his path up the dungeon staircase, Brom returned to the warlord's chamber. Grigori's daughter, Serena, knelt beside her father as he lay before the hearth. Smoke from the dungeon fire had begun to filter up into the higher regions of the castle.

Grigori forced a smile as he saw Brom approach. "You

have severed the serpent's head," the old man said. "The great beast has been vanquished."

Brom stepped to Grigori's side. "And what of Ramiel's soldiers?"

"You have slain their master," the seer whispered. "They have fled the castle to escape your wrath."

Brom knelt beside the dying man.

Grigori coughed, trying to clear his throat of blood. "You are a man of honor, Lord Brom. I have instructed Serena to trust in you. She shall relay the scroll's message to you once you have delivered her to safety."

Brom looked into Serena's tearful eyes. "No harm shall come to her," he said softly. "I shall protect her with my life."

The seer took a gasping breath and gazed into the fire once more. Brom clutched the dying man's hand to share his final vision. A barrage of hellish images flooded Brom's thoughts. Fire blazed atop a mountain summit amidst a shower of molten sparks and a billowing tower of smoke. A dark form rose from the flames, spreading ebon wings to eclipse the light of the dawning day. The ominous shadow opened its eyes, then slowly lifted its head, revealing its face to the world.

As Brom stared into the eyes of the beast, a newfound terror gripped his heart. For as he gazed upon the diabolic visage of the demon, Brom recognized the cruel face that stared back. It was not the face of the Dark Queen, Mara, nor her ruthless minion Dravek. The face of the rising beast was none other than his own.

Index: Artwork by Joseph Vargo

JOSEPH VARGO resides in Cleveland, Ohio where he has been conjuring fantasy artwork professionally since 1986. His gothic images open a gateway to the darkside and dare the viewer to venture within. Joseph's haunting visions of fantasy and horror have appeared in numerous publications, and his lithographs, printwear and Gothic Tarot deck are distributed worldwide. His artbook, *Born of the Night: The Gothic Fantasy Artwork of Joseph Vargo,* features a collection of over 100 paintings and illustrations spanning 20 years of his career. Joseph is also a noted composer and musician, earning worldwide acclaim with his musical project Nox Arcana. His book *The Legend of Darklore Manor and Other Tales of Terror* contains 13 sinister stories including the novella that chronicles the grim history of the haunted mansion that inspired Nox Arcana's debut album.

Joseph Iorillo is a freelance writer living in Cleveland Heights, Ohio. He is a *Summa Cum Laude* graduate of John Carroll University and holds a Bachelor of Arts degree in English. As a staff writer for *Dark Realms Magazine,* Joseph contributed numerous articles on topics as diverse as secret societies, ancient Sumeria, horror cinema, haunted houses and theories of the afterlife. Joseph has written several mystery and suspense novels, including the contemporary ghost story *This House Is Empty Now.* He is the co-author of *The Gothic Tarot Compendium* and *The Legend of Darklore Manor and Other Tales of Terror.* Joseph holds a lifelong interest in the esoteric mysteries of the world as well as all things supernatural. Visit Joseph's official website at: *www.JosephIorillo.com*

THE LEGEND OF DARKLORE MANOR AND OTHER TALES OF TERROR

Enter a dark realm of living gargoyles, sinister shadows, diabolical dolls, haunted havens and undead nightmares in this illustrated anthology of thirteen tales by Joseph Vargo and Joseph Iorillo, including the original novella inspired by Nox Arcana's haunting concept album, *Darklore Manor*.

THE DARK TOWER BOOK SERIES

The Dark Tower saga begins with thirteen illustrated tales of gothic mystery, horror and romance. Discover the origins of the sinister tower and the tragic souls cursed to forever haunt its forsaken halls.

THE DARK TOWER SOUNDTRACK BY NOX ARCANA

21 tracks of haunting melodies, ominous orchestrations and chilling sound effects provide the perfect atmosphere of mystery and menace for *The Dark Tower* book series. Composed by Joseph Vargo.

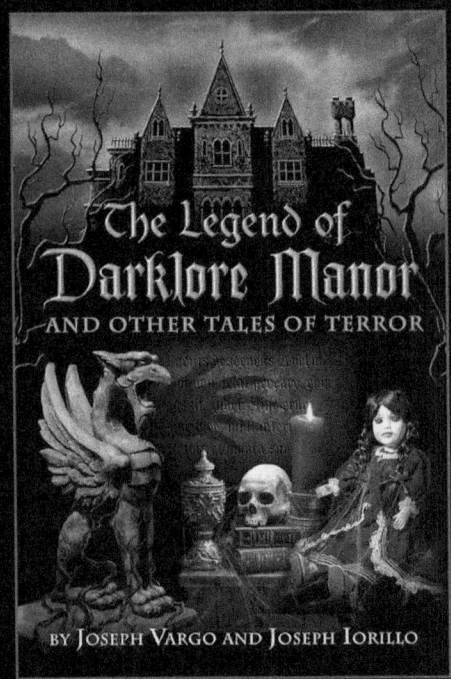

www.ingramcontent.com/pod-product-compliance
Lightning Source LLC
Chambersburg PA
CBHW051644260626
47170CB00004B/1318